THE SPIRIT of the FOYLE

About the Author

Mary Regan was born on a farm in County Derry but she has spent most of her life in Derry city. She lived for four years in England before returning to Derry where she now teaches in a primary school. Recently she was awarded a Master's Degree from the University of Ulster.

Her interests include folklore, archaeology and drama and she enjoys combining history with a touch of mystery. Donegal is one of her favourite places and she spends her summers in a caravan there. She is married with four children.

THE SPIRIT of the FOYLE

∾ **MARY REGAN** ∾

Book Two in the Brod of Bres Trilogy

POOLBEG

Published in 1994 by
Poolbeg Press Ltd,
Knocksedan House,
123 Baldoyle Industrial Estate,
Dublin 13, Ireland

© Mary Regan 1994

The moral right of the author has been asserted.

The financial assistance of the Arts Council of Northern Ireland
is gratefully acknowledged.

A catalogue record for this book is available from the British Library.

ISBN 1 85371 431 3

Cover illustration by Jane Doran,
Cover design by Poolbeg Group Services Ltd
Set by Poolbeg Group Services Ltd in Rotis Serif 10/13.5
Printed by The Guernsey Press Ltd,
Vale, Guernsey, Channel Islands.

For Dearbhla

Contents

✎ The Announcement ✎

"You look as happy as a turkey at Christmas," grinned Hugh Bradley as he saw his grandson's glum face across the breakfast table. "Come on, nothing can be that bad!"

Robin Drake smiled. His grandfather always managed to cheer him up but he still hated school – especially on Monday mornings.

"Get a move on, Robin, or you'll be late for the bus again," scolded his mother as she reached him his packed lunch. Silently the boy pushed the lunch into his bag, then he said his good-byes and left for another day in the school in Drumenny village.

"I worry about him, daddy," said Rosaleen Drake as she watched her son's hunched back disappear out the gate. "I think he's not happy here but he never says anything."

"Give him a bit more time, Rosaleen love. It's only been a wheen of months. He'll settle. Robin's got plenty of backbone in him."

"I hope you're right," sighed his daughter as she began to clear the table. "He misses his dad terrible."

Hugh Bradley knew that Robin missed his father and that he was very unhappy since his parents had separated. Life had not dealt kindly with the boy in his short eleven years. Robin had been brought up in family quarters in army camps in England and Germany and then suddenly, six months ago, he had found himself on the side of a lonely Irish mountain with only his mother and an old man for company.

"It's all my fault," said Rosaleen miserably. "Maybe I should have let him stay in England when he was over with his granny after Christmas."

"Look, Rosaleen," said Hugh rising from the table. "Robin's father can't live here and you found you couldn't live there. It's not a great situation for the boy. He loves the both of you but he made the decision to come here. Now we have to help him and long faces won't do it."

At the fork in the lane Robin waited. A blur of purple and pink hurtled towards him as Aileen Kennedy arrived, late and dishevelled as usual.

"I can't find my homework book anywhere," panted the girl. "Mrs Mac'll kill me."

"I know where it is," said Robin as he hurried her along the lane.

"Where?"

"In my bag."

"How did it get there?"

"You did your homework in my house on Friday night."

"So I did!" exploded Aileen. "I'm the right thicko. I forgot all about it and I have my room nearly torn apart."

"Homework out," said Mrs McCloskey and Aileen was very relieved as she placed her books on the desk for the teacher's temper was not the best on a Monday morning. There was a fistling and fuffling beside her.

"What's the matter?" she asked as Robin searched frantically through his school bag.

"It's not here," he said.

"What?"

"My homework book."

"But it must be. I saw it when you gave me mine on the bus."

"Well it's not here now," said Robin in a resigned voice and he put his bag on the floor.

Aileen looked around the room and her heart sank. Something was being passed from table to table. Lisa McCarron nudged Nuala Deery and Nuala slid the red exercise book on to the girl in front. Robin sat with a face of stone although he knew perfectly well what was happening.

"Now," said Mrs McCloskey, "I gave you some work on area and volume to do over the weekend. We'll get the answers first and then I'll come round and see the books."

Some of the children were reluctant to pass Robin's book round but no one was prepared to stand up to the Battler Gang. For this was the work of Battler Doherty and his cronies, Ronan McCafferty and Wee Willie Clements.

"What do you mean, you can't find it?" asked Mrs McCloskey as she drummed a finger nail on Robin's desk. Robin didn't answer.

"Did you do your homework Robin Drake?"

"Yes I did Miss."

"And did you put your book into your bag?"

"Yes, Miss."

"And it has disappeared?"

3

"Yes."

"Well now, Robin, how do you explain that mystery?"

The boy stood pale and unflinching before the teacher but he remained silent. Mrs McCloskey was perplexed. A missing book was a common occurrence when homework wasn't done but since Robin Drake had joined the class he had always turned in his work. There were unpleasant undercurrents in the class which she sensed but couldn't pin down. They had been there all year and seemed to centre round those two loners, Robin Drake and Aileen Kennedy. The Drake boy especially was a bit of an outsider. The teacher sighed. This had been a difficult year so far and it wasn't getting any better.

"I have no doubt you will find you have left the book at home. Bring it in tomorrow and I will check both sets of work."

Battler Doherty was a bit disappointed that Robin didn't get more of a chewing up but he enjoyed sitting back in his chair as the teacher cast an approving glance at the homework that did not belong to him.

At lunch time Aileen and Robin found the book as they were throwing the remains of their lunches into the bin in the playground. They dug it out from under apple stumps and half-eaten sandwiches. It was covered in the sticky tops of yoghurt cartons and the dregs of flasks.

"Why didn't you tell her?" asked Aileen. "Why didn't you say Battler Doherty had your book?"

Robin shrugged his shoulders and his face was closed and expressionless. There were times when she just didn't understand Robin Drake at all. She'd had more than her share of torment from Battler and his hangers on but she shouted back; she gave as good as she got. Robin Drake just sat with a face like stone and said nothing. Yet he wasn't a coward; she knew that for a fact.

After lunch Mrs McCloskey came bustling into the room clutching a sheaf of papers. Two bright pink spots of excitement burned in her cheeks.

"I have a great piece of news!" she gushed breathlessly. "Drumenny School has been specially chosen to take part in a big pageant to be held in Derry on St Patrick's Day. It is part of the Spirit of the Foyle Festival which will celebrate the River Foyle and all the history it has seen. There will be street carnivals and bands and then the chosen schools will act out different periods of history showing the importance of the river to the life of the people. There will be Viking warriors, missionary monks, Irish chieftains, English grandees, Scottish settlers, hungry emigrants and even American naval personnel! There will be a parade of boats from every century and at the end of all the festivities a special statue called 'The Spirit of the Foyle' will be put in place right in the middle of the river in memory of all who have sailed in or out of the Foyle and to welcome visitors to the city. The whole thing will be rounded off with a fantastic fireworks display."

The class greeted this announcement with a total lack of enthusiasm but Mrs McCloskey didn't seem to notice. "As this is your last year in the school, Mr Quinn has decided that this class will do the Live History performance. Each chosen school has been allocated a particular historical period and we will be

Stone Age farmers."

A groan went up from the class.

"Why can't we be Vikings, Miss?" demanded Battler Doherty. "We could wear helmets with horns and long moustaches and have swords and all."

The teacher sighed. "Another school has been chosen to be Vikings," she explained patiently, "and besides, it is highly unlikely that the Vikings ever wore horned helmets. The Neolithic people – the Stone Age farmers – are a far more interesting group. We have a lot of work ahead of us but it will be worth it in the end. We will make our own costumes and they will be authentic. I'm sure any of your fathers who are farmers will give us some sheep skins or goat skins and some raw wool. We will learn how to spin the wool the way they did it then and we will make looms to weave the rough material that was made into garments . . . "

"Yuck!" said Lisa McCarron in disgust. "I'm not wearing an old home-made sack or rotten goat skin. It'll be wild itchy!"

"And it'll stink too!" added Nuala Deery.

"We'll discuss costumes later," said Mrs McCloskey, "but you certainly won't be wearing those earrings, Miss McCarron!"

Lisa tossed her head and flicked the dangling strands of beads and coloured feathers that sprouted from her ears.

"Starting right now," continued the teacher, "I think we should do some work on the Stone Age farmers. We really need to get some background knowledge before we can compose an accurate scene from their everyday lives."

Tasks and lists of books to look up in the library

were handed out to the uninterested pupils and names of parents who might be willing to help were taken. Ronan McCafferty stretched out a leg to nudge Battler Doherty's sturdy ankle with a thick soled boot.

"This stupid oul' carry on had better not interfere with the match," he whispered. Battler raised a thumb and cocked an eyebrow.

"Dead right!" he said and beside him Wee Willie Clements nodded in silent agreement. Drumenny had climbed successfully up the Interschools Football League table and the final was always played on the 18th of March, the day after St Patrick's Day. Nothing would be allowed to take precedence over the football!

∾ The Stone House of the Sun ∾

"Take those with you and put them under the front seat of the bus," said Mrs McCloskey as she reached a sheaf of plastic bags to the first child who came to hand.

"Bags! What do we want with plastic bags?" demanded the headmaster.

"They're sick bags," muttered Mrs McCloskey. She began to distribute clipboards and pencils.

"Sick bags!" bellowed Mr Quinn. "What would we be needing sick bags for? Aren't we only going a couple of miles up the road? We're not taking any babies with us are we?"

A frown creased the teacher's face but she said nothing; nothing out loud, that is. She wished now that she had never told Mr Quinn about the trip to the old stone fort at the top of Grianan Hill. Normally the headmaster did not go on school outings but, as he fancied himself a bit of an expert on local history, he was taking the opportunity to conduct the tour of the Grianan of Aileach personally. He was organising and bawling instructions at the top of his famous voice and all was confusion and chaos in the classroom.

It had come as a shock to Mrs McCloskey to discover that although Grianan Hill overlooked the village of Drumenny and could be seen from her classroom window, only a couple of children had actually been up to the ancient stone fort at its crown. St Patrick himself had visited the fort and kings had been crowned there for centuries. The Grianan of Aileach means the Stone house of the Sun and historians believe that the hill was a place of pagan worship even in Stone Age times, long before the stone fort was built by the Celts. So, as part of the class work on the Stone Age farmers, Mrs McCloskey decided to pay a visit to the Grianan of Aileach. It had been a spur of the moment idea; one which the harassed teacher now thought she should have buried.

Mr Quinn wasn't a bad sort as headmasters go, but he did like to be in charge and in Mrs McCloskey's opinion he couldn't organise a bun fight in a bakery. She was going to have to listen to that voice all day too. It would boom in her ear until her head was ready for blast off. The headmaster's nickname was Lambeg and it was a good choice. The Lambeg is a huge drum with a boom so loud that it is said it can be heard for ten miles or more.

The battered bus creaked and groaned up the steep, crazily winding road and lurched to a halt in a small tarred area that served as a car park. The door of the bus opened and a noisy clutch of anoraked and wellie-booted mini-gangsters tumbled out on to the blustery hillside and prepared to tackle the very steep slope up to the fort.

For a few moments the children were struck dumb when they emerged from the short stone tunnel at the entrance to the fort. It was not just the stiff climb that had robbed them of breath, it was the size of the fort inside that made them gape in silent awe. The great walls rose in stepped rings, higher than two triple-decker buses. The floor was grass-covered but there were the charred remains of fires that had warmed summertime campers.

The silence didn't last too long and soon bodies were clambering up steps and over ledges to reach the stone platform that ran around the top of the wall, or bottoms were disappearing into holes that tunnelled into the ramparts. Up at the very top Lambeg was singing the praises of the magnificent view that could be seen if only the clouds hadn't blotted it out. He then began a running commentary on the history of the Grianan of Aileach from pagan times when tools were made of stone and the sun was worshipped, to Christian times when battles were fought and kings were crowned. But there was nobody to listen to Lambeg except a few cows grazing on the lower slopes and they scampered off, frightened by the monster roaring from the battlements.

Things were not going well for Mrs McCloskey. She had sent a group off with tapes to measure the outer rings, the remains of old defence ditches, that surrounded the fort. One of the party had gone knee-deep into black, glarry bog muck and another had slid into a fresh pat of cow dung. Battler Doherty, who was the scourge of her life, had discovered a well behind the fort that was full of ten, twenty and even the odd fifty pence luck pieces. It was Wee Willie Clements's luck that Battler chose him to be lowered down to plunder the treasure.

Willie now stood before his dismayed teacher and he was drenched. The water dripped from his soaked anorak into his squelchy boots and his hair was plastered to his skull in a slimy green mess. The skinny Neptune wept dirty brown tears and shivered in his wet clothes.

Aileen Kennedy and Robin Drake had slipped off to explore on their own and hoped that they wouldn't be noticed – particularly by Battler Doherty and his cronies.

"Is this the place then?" asked Robin. "Is this where the Brod of Bres is now?"

Aileen nodded and her long fair hair streamed back in the wind. "It all seems like a dream now doesn't it? I mean, it's hard to believe it all really happened." Aileen's thoughts had drifted miles and months away, back to the day she found the little two-faced figure, the Brod of Bres, hidden among the seaweed on the beach. The Brod had let her into many adventures in worlds that lie hidden within our own and she supposed it was really responsible for her friendship with Robin Drake.

"What do you think they would say if we told them that deep in the heart of this hill a band of warriors lies sleeping waiting for the gods to call them to battle?" she asked smiling.

"I don't think they would believe us somehow," chuckled Robin. "How could anything be asleep with Lambeg thundering away up there?"

Aileen laughed but then she grew solemn.

"I'm glad the Brod is in there with them, out of harm's way."

"You mean out of the Morrigan's way," said Robin and they both shivered at the memory of the evil creature who could change shape in a flash and whose greatest desire was to possess the Brod of Bres, the key to unlimited power.

"Lunch time!" called Mrs McCloskey and a hungry horde descended on the boxes of packed lunches. By the time Aileen and Robin got there, there were no buns or apples left. Battler Doherty stood grinning at them with his mouth full and his pockets bulging, daring them to complain.

"Come on," said Aileen turning away from his ugly leer. "Aggie Scroggy baked this morning and I've got plenty in my bag."

Robin's mouth watered at the thought of Aggie's delicious apple tart and he followed Aileen as she climbed right up to the top of the fort. They sat on the broad wall, eating and looking at the scene spread in front of them. The clouds had lifted and the sun was beginning to break through in broad shafts, lighting the countryside like torch beams in a cinema.

"It's fabulous," said Robin appreciating the view. Below them Lough Swilly stretched to the sea and over to the right they could see the waters of Lough Foyle and the smoky haze of Derry city.

"There's Cloughderg Mountain," said Aileen indicating the hill with its stone finger pointing at the sky.

"I can see our house," said Robin, "and yours too. Here have a look."

Robin passed his powerful binoculars to Aileen and she strained to find the Scroggy farm where she now lived. At first she could see nothing but Robin showed her how to adjust the focus and then she was amazed at how clearly she could see the little farm tucked under Cloughderg Mountain and perched above Lough Foyle.

Suddenly a powerful shove jolted Aileen forward

and the binoculars flew out of her hands. Luckily they were still looped round Robin's neck or they would have gone crashing down and would have been smashed against the scattered stones that littered the ground below. The huge bulk of Battler Doherty pinned them in against the wall.

"Give us a look," said Battler grabbing for the glasses.

"No," said Robin quietly but defiantly.

Aileen's heart thumped. Robin's huge brown eyes glinted angrily and there was a stubborn set to his small pale face. Ronan McCafferty and Wee Willie Clements stood on either side of Battler and it was clear they were looking for trouble.

"Army issue, are they then?" sneered Ronan. "Brit property?"

"Hand them over," demanded Battler and tugged at the binoculars.

"No," said Robin again and he clung on to the strap although he was almost strangling.

"Stop it, you rotten bully," shouted Aileen and she punched Battler's well padded arm. He didn't even flinch. He began to twist the strap until it was biting cruelly into Robin's neck.

"Give them to me!"

Robin shook his head defiantly. Battler twisted again and Robin's face began to go blue. He was having difficulty breathing.

"Do what he says!" urged Aileen in panic but Robin stubbornly stood his ground. Aileen knew that neither Battler Doherty nor Robin Drake would give in and she was terrified.

"Ronan, Colm, come down here," called Mrs

McCloskey. "I want you to carry the boxes back to the bus." Aileen almost fainted with relief.

Battler scowled but he did not let go of the strap.

"Now, Colm," insisted the teacher looking up from the floor of the fort.

"You'd better go," panted Robin in a husky voice. "The teacher wants you, Colm."

Battler's face turned purple with anger. He loathed his proper name almost as much as he loathed this boy with the poncy accent. "Shut your face, smart ass," he growled.

"Colm Doherty. I mean NOW!"

Battler gave another vicious twist to the strap. Then, reluctantly, he let it go and turned to climb back down the steps to the waiting teacher. "I'll get you again, Chookie Birdie. You're dead – and you too, Alien," he hissed before his head disappeared over the edge of the platform.

"Phew!" sighed Aileen in relief. "One more twist of that strap and you'd have been a dead duck." The two burst out laughing at Aileen's choice of words. Robin Drake's name was a source of great amusement in Drumenny School and was the reason for the nickname that Battler had thrown at him.

Mrs McCloskey looked up when she heard the laughter. She sensed that something unpleasant had been happening up on the walls and she felt uneasy. Aileen Kennedy and Robin Drake always seemed to be at the mercy of Battler Doherty and his gang but they never came to her with any complaints. At least the two were good friends and if they had a problem they seemed to be coping with it. She would be glad when June came and this lot would be out of her life and into their secondary school.

"Did you see his face when you called him Colm?" chortled Aileen.

"Yeah," smiled Robin. "Now I know how to really annoy him."

"Do you know what Colm means – in Irish?"

Robin shook his head.

"It means dove, the dove of peace."

Another ripple of explosive laughter from the top of the fort set the teacher at ease and further enraged Battler Doherty.

At about half past two Lambeg decided that even he'd had enough and so he organised a litter hunt before setting off back to Drumenny. Bedraggled hunters were trailing bags of rubbish back to the bus under the eagle eye of Lambeg when a battered yellow van trundled up the hill and came to a stop a few feet away from the bus. The back doors opened and two men in dungarees began to unload equipment. They had all sorts of gadgets, including tape measures and stands with three legs and a thing like a telescope on the top. The driver was wearing a suit under his heavy anorak and he seemed to be in charge. The three went into a conference huddle and there was much peering through the glass and taking of notes.

Lambeg could not contain his curiosity. He strode over to the group to find out what they were up to. The children waiting to board the bus could not hear what the men were saying but they did not have to strain at all to catch Lambeg's remarks.

"Heritage Centre!" he bawled. "Cafés and souvenir shops and hordes of people trampling all over Aileach of the Kings! We'll see about that!" He threatened to organise petitions and campaigns and protest marches and promised a sorry end to anyone who dared to desecrate the sacred soil of Grianan.

"You don't know who you're dealing with when you're up against me," he shouted at the bewildered survey team. "There'll be no bulldozers on Grianan Hill churning up thousands of years of history!"

Robin and Aileen exchanged alarmed glances. Aileen thought of the Brod of Bres safe in the cave of the slumbering warriors and a worm of worry ate into her heart.

Mrs McCloskey's head was thumping. A screeched chorus, threatening to hang all and sundry from the sour apple tree, was blasting from the back of the bus and the headmaster was bouncing his temper off her ear drums. She sympathised with Mr Quinn's dismay but she had heard quite enough about vandals in hard hats and money makers with no souls. She wished with all her heart that the headmaster had an 'off' button that she could push.

The bus lurched over a vicious bump in the road and suddenly Mr Quinn's tirade was cut off in mid-sentence. His red face paled rapidly and a greenish tinge began to creep around his cheeks. Quickly Mrs McCloskey reached under the seat. For the rest of the journey back to Drumenny village Lambeg kept his head buried in the plastic bag and Mrs McCloskey only had to listen to thirty-five rowdies.

༄ At Home ༄

Later that evening Robin and Aileen walked along the narrow lane that meandered up towards Cloughderg Mountain and then they stood talking at the fork that took them their separate ways to their homes.

"I thought we would never have to worry about it again," said Aileen. "It was supposed to be safe there forever."

"Well," said Robin, "you remember what Mathgen said about nothing being certain any more once the Brod was disturbed the first time?"

"Mmm . . . " said Aileen and she was thinking about the old man they had meet in the woods – Mathgen, the Chief Druid to the Children of Danu.

"Mathgen was right about people anyway," she said. "Mortals do mess everything up. Should we try to find him and tell him what is happening at Grianan?"

Robin thought for a while and then he shook his head. "I don't think so. He hates any contact from our world at all. Anyway, Lambeg is likely to put a stop to the whole business."

"He could stop a stampeding herd of elephants if he put his mind to it," smiled Aileen.

"Or his voice," replied Robin. "We'll leave it for now. If Lambeg does get a campaign going, we can help and

17

if anything happens we'll know about it."

It was five months since the Brod of Bres had first led the children to Mathgen and his Otherworld. Then they had listened enthralled as the old man told them about the war between the evil Fomar people and the Children of the goddess Danu; a war that had been going on since long before a mortal foot trod the soil of Ireland. Bres, whose mother had been of the Danu people and whose father was a king of the Fomar, had betrayed the Danu and they became slaves to the Fomar and their wicked monsters. After many trials and long suffering the Danu finally faced up to Balor of the Evil Eye, the gigantic god of the Fomar whose one eye possessed all the evil that had ever been known.

The gods of Light had come to the aid of the Children of Danu and both Balor and Bres had been turned to stone. Balor's head had been severed from his shoulders by the mighty Caladbolg, the Sword of Light, and was now lost among the craggy hills around the country. The Morrigan, the Fomar sorceress, eternally sought the Evil Eye so that she could have for herself that terrible power. The Brod of Bres was the key that would open the eye and unleash all the destructive power on all the worlds. It was Mathgen's job to see that the Brod was well guarded so that even if the Morrigan found the Evil Eye she would be powerless without the little two-faced statue.

After the last great battle, the Brod had been given into the safekeeping of Manaanan Mac Lir, the sea-god who lived in the deep waters at the mouth of the Foyle. The god had grown careless and after a fierce storm Aileen had found the Brod on the beach below her

house. From then on she too was part of the war. The
Morrigan, and the horrible creatures who were her
slaves in the Underworld, had taken the Brod from
Aileen and had almost taken her life.

In a night filled with danger and terror the Brod had
been rescued and the Danu had sent it into the cavern
deep under Grianan Hill where a band of slumbering
warriors awaited the call of the gods to battle.

"I've just cleaned that, you vandal," said his mother
when Robin plastered his face up against the kitchen
window, "get in here 'til I give you a good hiding."

Robin jumped down off the upturned bucket and
went inside. His mother was washing dishes and she
squirted the soapy water at him.

"An ill-reared brat you are."

"Thank you kindly, ma'am," replied Robin pulling a
face. Rosaleen Drake laughed and dried her hands.

"How did the trip go?"

"Oh, all right."

"All right. Well that tells me a lot."

"Where's Granda?" asked Robin.

"Where do you think?" replied his mother.

"I'll go out to him, then."

"Give me those binoculars before you go. I'll put
them away."

Rosaleen watched as her son ran towards the shed
where his grandfather spent most of his waking hours
tinkering with anything electrical from toasters to
milking machines. Then she lifted the case with the
powerful binoculars and went into the back room to
put them with the other gear that Robin's father had
given him. There were torches, compasses, a good

camera, a tent in a bag and all sorts of camping gear. It was all good stuff, the sort of equipment a soldier would have.

Carefully she packed away the binoculars. The room was not a bit like Robin's bedroom back in England. It looked bare and unlived in like a room in a boarding house. No personal possessions cluttered shelves or tumbled off the top of the wardrobe. All Robin's favourite things were still in cardboard boxes as if he felt it wasn't worth while unpacking – he wouldn't be staying that long.

Rosaleen opened one of the boxes and smiled. It was jammed full of football souvenirs. An autographed picture of the Red Devils – the Manchester United team – was carefully rolled in a cardboard tube alongside badges and banners and mementoes of every game he had attended at the Old Trafford stadium. His red and white strip was there along with his hat and scarf. Four scrap books bulging with newspaper cuttings took up most of the space in the box and under them Rosaleen found Robin's own trophies and medals.

Before their return to Ireland Rosaleen and her son had settled in Manchester near Robin's English grandparents and for two years he had gone to school there. It was in this school that his special talent had been discovered. Robin Drake was a brilliant footballer and twice he had been chosen as the footballer of the year in the Greater Manchester Junior League. In England Robin had lived, breathed and dreamed nothing but football. Since coming to Cloughderg he had never mentioned it.

Voices coming across the yard from the shed roused Rosaleen out of her musings and she went out to greet her father and her son.

"Did you hear this, Rosaleen," called Hugh Bradley, "there's big plans to turn Grianan into a tourist centre. There'll be ski-lifts and night clubs and casinos galore. We'll be up to our oxters in film stars and royalty!"

Rosaleen laughed, "And an aerodrome too I suppose, you oul' eejit."

"Would you listen to that for respect! That's the sort of behaviour she learnt in England is it?" said Hugh mournfully to his grandson. Robin was grinning broadly. At first he had been confused by his grandfather's banter but now he knew that the straighter Hugh Bradley kept his face the more he was taking the mickey.

"I can't imagine who she learnt it from, Granda," he said innocently. "She was always like that."

Hugh Bradley threw back his head and crowed in delight. Then he put an arm round his daughter's shoulders. "You have a right one there, Rosaleen," he said. "Between the two of you you'll have me kilt."

In the Scroggy house Aileen too was talking to her mother. "Where is everybody?" she asked.

"They're up in the field. One of the ewes is having a bad time and I'm not much use when it comes to the lambing."

'Everybody' was Tom Scroggy and his mother, Aggie. Claire Kennedy, Aileen's mother, had married Tom suddenly and secretly one morning and Aileen's life was turned inside out. Her father had died when Aileen was a baby and she grew up with her mother in the village of Drumenny. When her mother remarried without telling her, she felt betrayed and cheated. To

21

make matters worse, the Scroggys, especially Aggie, were considered to be a bit odd. In school Aileen had become 'The Alien' and was mocked mercilessly. She missed living in the village and did not like Cloughderg Mountain one little bit.

At first she loathed and distrusted Aggie but now she had learned to respect her. In her quiet withdrawn way she was kind and, as it turned out, she proved to be very useful when the Morrigan had used trickery to capture Aileen and the Brod of Bres. Still, Aileen was not completely at ease on the Scroggy farm and often wished that she was still living in the flat above the chemist shop in Drumenny.

"What are you doing?" asked Aileen.

"I'm getting the four o'clock tea ready to take up to them."

"Do you want me to take it up?"

Claire glanced quickly at her daughter and her eyes lit up with approval. Aileen really had been trying hard to be pleasant recently. She was no longer the scowling, silent monster who never spoke to Tom if she could help it and who looked at Aggie as if she had just crawled out of a hole.

"Would you, love? That would be great. I could get on with the dinner then."

On a flattish grassy part of the hillside, Tom Scroggy had created a shelter of sorts with bales of hay and it was there that Aileen found himself and Aggie.

"How's she doing?" she asked as she unpacked the flask and the food.

"She's not great," said Tom and he shook his head and looked worried. Mountain weather had creased and buffed his face to a healthy red-brown sheen and his thick greying hair was stuck to his forehead with sweat. "I think I'm going to have to get her into the barrow and take her down to the house. This is a job for the vet."

"We'll have a sup of tea first," said Aggie handing over a steaming mug. The old woman looked tired and Aileen guessed they had been working with the ewe for hours. "Did you have a nice day at Grianan?" asked Aggie as she sipped the hot tea gratefully.

"It was all right."

A coarse squawk startled Tom as he was about to bite into a scone.

"Gerrourathat!" he shouted and he flicked a stone expertly.

"Scavenging beast," muttered Aggie and then she saw how deathly pale Aileen had gone. "Don't be worrying yourself, Aileen," she said and she touched her shoulder gently. "It's the lambs that one is after. It has nothing to do with you."

What Aggie said made sense but still Aileen looked fearfully over her shoulder to the rock where the hooded crow had flown out of the range of Tom's stones. It was just an ordinary grey crow. Big, ugly, fierce and looking for a handy meal. It could not be the crow that had lured Aileen to the Pit of the Hell Hag and then had changed into the terrible beauty – the Morrigan – the Shape-shifter.

∽ Under the Hill of Grianan ∽

It was a Saturday morning and Lambeg had organised a protest march against the building of a Heritage Centre at Grianan Hill. Almost everybody in and around the village was going. Not all were in total agreement with the protest, indeed quite a few thought a Heritage Centre would bring some tourists and their welcome wallets to the area, but many had been taught by Lambeg and were still slightly in awe of him. Besides it was a day out and there was likely to be a bit of crack.

"Go you with them, Tom," said Aggie Scroggy. "I'll look after things here. All the ewes are in the pen and sure there's none of them due to lamb just yet."

Reluctantly Tom Scroggy agreed to go. He didn't give a tuppenny hoot about the whole business but there wasn't enough room in Hugh Bradley's van for people and banners so Tom's battered car was needed. It had been a terrible rush getting the feeding and the milking done but by half past nine they were ready to go. Aileen travelled in the van with Robin and the banners, and Rosaleen Drake went in the car with Claire and Tom Scroggy.

It was a bitterly cold morning and Cloughderg Mountain was powdered in snow. The road into the village was clear but it was treacherously icy in parts. The car park outside the Drumenny Community Centre was packed with vehicles parked higgledy-piggledy all over the place. Inside there was even more confusion. Lambeg was hollering instructions but not too many were listening to him. Some people hadn't seen other people since Christmas and there was a lot of news to pass around.

Eventually a cavalcade of cars, vans and motorbikes left the village and headed towards the Grianan of Aileach. The story of the climb to the top of the hill would be told in shop, chapel and pub for many months to come. Wise owls parked at the bottom of the hill and went up the icy slope on foot but the foolhardy drove on. After a lot of sliding and slipping and vehicles going into ditches, Lambeg at last managed to assemble his followers in the small car park below the fort.

"Now," he said, "the JCBs are here but we are going to stop them by fair means or foul. We'll line up and stand in front of them with our banners." Off he strode at the head of his band of obedient disciples as they held the banners aloft.

"CLEAR OFF! CLEAR OFF!" he chanted thumping the air with his fist.

A few half-heartedly joined in but their voices were not needed. Lambeg's roar was more than enough.

There was really not very much to protest at. There were two JCBs on the hill all right but one was silent and stationary and the other was bogged down.

"CLEAR OFF!" Lambeg roared at the man on the paralysed digger. "THIS IS SACRED GROUND. CLEAR OFF!"

"I wish to God I could," answered the frustrated driver. "Am I in deep at the back?" Lambeg could never resist an appeal for an opinion.

"You're not too bad," he shouted when he had examined the damage. "Come on you boys, we'll soon have it out."

Reluctantly, a few of the men shuffled forward. It seemed to them that if Lambeg wanted to stop the work then the JCB would best be left up to its axles in the bog. Some grumbled but none was prepared to challenge the headmaster.

"Get in there and put your backs to it," ordered Lambeg and a half dozen or so obeyed him.

"FIRE AWAY!" he roared

The driver switched on his engine and the huge back wheels of the JCB whirred. The men put their shoulders to the massive digger.

"HEAVE!" urged Lambeg.

The giant tyres whirred and stuck and then began to churn. A stream of black glar spewed out from under each wheel. Lambeg and the volunteers were plastered in a thick layer of sacred ground. It took a while to scrape some of the muck off and to reorganise the protest. This time Lambeg led his band towards a group of workers in helmets. They were clustered round the other JCB and seemed to be examining something on the side of the hill.

"Who's in charge here?" demanded Lambeg. "I want to speak to the man in charge."

"What is it you want?" asked one of the men.

"Are you the foreman?"

"Yeah."

"Well, I wish to inform you that we are the

Drumenny Heritage Protection Group and we are determined to stop all work here today."

"Is that a fact?"

"It is. We are prepared to lie down in front of your machines if needs be. Men, women and, yes, even the children will defy you. These machines will not dig another sod this day."

"You're right there," said the man in the helmet. "There'll be no more digging done here today."

For a very short space of time, Lambeg was lost for words. Then he found them again.

"YOU MEAN WE HAVE WON?" he bellowed. "DRUMENNY HAS BEATEN THE PLANNERS AND THE BUREAUCRATS?"

"Well, I don't know who has beaten who," said the man, "but we can dig no further. We've dug into a dirty great tunnel or something. This side of the hill is in a very dangerous condition. It could cave in at any time. So I am calling a halt to all the work until I get some experts on the scene."

There was nothing left for the protest group to protest about so they unpacked the flasks and sandwiches they had brought with them and shared their picnic with the workmen.

Aileen and Robin slipped away and stood looking into the black hole that the digger had unearthed. They couldn't see very far into the tunnel but it seemed to be lined with stones as big as a standing man.

"Do you think this is the place?" breathed Aileen. "Are the warriors sleeping in there?"

"Could be anything," said Robin.

"Come away from there you two! That could go at any time."

Robin turned to obey the foreman's shouted instruction and Aileen turned too. Then she turned back again. She never could explain later why she did what she did. She only knew that something drew her into that tunnel.

It was a fairly narrow corridor, paved top, bottom and sides with huge slab stones. Some of the slabs were carved in weird patterns of circles within circles and diamond shapes and spirals. Others had rows of zigzag lines or clusters of small suns with rays joining up like a game of join the dots. But soon she could see nothing at all and was feeling her way gingerly along the cold rough walls. The tunnel began to dip slightly and then, away in the distance, she could see a haze of light. It was not the cold light of day. It was a low, flickering glow; the light of warmth and welcome.

The tunnel came to an abrupt and dramatic halt. Aileen stood poised on a small platform that hung over a room carved out of solid rock. Firebrands flared and spat in their brackets high up on the lofty wall. Tendrils of smoke drifted and curled between light and shadow. The walls of the cavern were draped with hangings, fringed and woven into scenes where fantastic animals prowled through forests of delicately beautiful trees and giant sized flowers bloomed in glorious colours.

The centre of the floor was taken up by a table, rough hewn out of a Goliath of a tree. The table was lighted with a host of thick yellow candles and heaved with an abundance of food. There were heads of pigs with apples in their mouths; sides of venison and crisp, roasted birds bigger than turkeys; glistening fish baked whole and dishes of eggs, blue, green and darkly speckled. Apples, plums and pears cascaded from tottering fruity mountains and flat loaves of dark bread sat in squat circles. Silver goblets brimmed with dark liquid and wooden plates lay empty and waiting. The food was steaming hot and the tempting aroma blended deliciously with the smell of candle wax.

All of this Aileen took in in a split second but almost immediately her astonished attention was riveted on the hulking slumbering bodies that lolled and curled on fleecy rugs around the full of the room. They were majestic in their snoring bliss. Taut muscles bulged from brawny arms and sprawled thighs. Riots of unruly hair, gold-red and jet black, were held in check by bands of beaten gold, and cloaks of red or deep purple covered short robes of milky white or pale saffron. Broad leather belts encircled thick waists where the jewelled hilts of broad-bladed swords peeped from leather scabbards. By each warrior's side lay a shield, heavily studded and laced with finely tooled designs. Beside each shield lay a sheaf of glinting spears.

A soft snuffling drew Aileen's attention to a dark corner of the room. Here an antechamber had been carved from the rock. It was spacious but low. In the gloom she saw horses. They were splendid. All were white with powerful muscles rippling under glossy coats. Silky manes, newly brushed and shining, rose and fell with the steady breathing of the animals. The horses stood sound asleep beside mangers filled with fresh sweet hay.

It has happened again, thought Aileen. I am back again in the Otherworld, the world that exists alongside our own in time and in space. Almost instinctively she looked for the Brod. Since she had first found the little statue she felt attached to it and now she sensed its

presence. The room was so big and the Brod so small –
only the length of her finger – that she thought she
would never see it. Her eyes scoured the walls, the roof,
the floor but it was not until she looked at the wall
above her head that she saw it. It was sitting
resplendent on a tiny altar that seemed to have been
carved specially from the hard rock face. If she
stretched a little she could touch it. She reached out.

A deep rumbling growl echoed round the cavern
and the ground shook. The warriors snorted and stirred
in their sleep. The horses shifted and pawed the ground.
Aileen held her breath and the slumberers settled and
rested easy again. The rumbling came again and dust
and fine rubble began to shower down. She put her
hands to the walls of the tunnel as if to steady them
but all around her a great disturbance heaved and
rippled. The tunnel was going to cave in! She would be
trapped! She fled along the stone-lined passage. The
walls vibrated and shifted and her hair and mouth were
filled with dust. She could not see a thing.

Outside on the slopes of Grianan the protesters too
had heard the rumble.

"Get everybody back in the vehicles," said the
foreman rising hastily to his feet. "I don't like the
sound of this."

"Aileen's not here," said Robin to his grandfather.

"What do you mean? Where is she?"

"I don't know," replied the frightened boy. "We were
looking into the tunnel and then we came away. I
thought she was right behind me."

Quickly Hugh ran to Tom Scroggy and told him
what he feared. Tom had been talking to Lambeg and
the three men scanned the crowd for Aileen's face and

then went towards the entrance to the tunnel.

"I told you to stay away from here," said the foreman.

"We think there is a child in the tunnel."

"My God!" said the man.

They stood peering into the murky gloom of the entrance while panic began to spread among the watchers as they counted heads. Claire Scroggy darted forward but Rosaleen Drake restrained her.

"Tom is there," she said. "She will be all right, Claire."

Robin had managed to stay beside his grandfather and he hooked himself into the comfort of his steady arm. Another great rumble came from inside the mountain and the watchers gasped in shock. Clouds of dust belched from the mouth of the tunnel.

Inside, Aileen was deafened by the noise. Behind her the tunnel shook and heaved and then collapsed in on itself in a thundering clatter of falling rock. Terror drove her forward through the choking dust and then she could see light. It was the entrance. She was almost there, she could make it!

"Aileen! Aileen Kennedy! Are you all right?" roared a terrified Lambeg into the black fog.

"For God's sake, don't shout!"

But the hissed warning came too late. Lambeg's blasting question rolled down the tunnel gaining in force as it bounced off the trembling walls. The tremors began afresh and just when Aileen thought she was safe the ground disappeared beneath her feet and she went tumbling into darkness.

❧ Drama and Courage ❧

Claire Scroggy screamed and broke loose from Rosaleen Drake's grip. She ran forward and only her husband's strong arms prevented her from plunging headlong into the wrecked tunnel.

"Wait, Claire! Wait! We don't know what's happened in there."

"Aileen's in there!" Claire screamed hysterically. "And we're standing here doing nothing!"

Robin hid his head in his grandfather's jacket and Hugh Bradley could feel him shake convulsively. There was nothing he could say to comfort his grandson. The shocked onlookers stood in stunned silence. Then a tiny sound was heard.

"Listen!" whispered Tom Scroggy. All prayed and strained to hear. The sound came again. It was thin and distant but it was unmistakably Aileen Kennedy's voice! The whole gathering heaved a sigh of relief.

When the dust settled Aileen found herself at the bottom of a deep shaft. Her head was spinning. She touched it and her fingers were damp and sticky. Every part of her body ached. Far above she could see daylight – the tunnel entrance. With a great effort she struggled to her feet and tried to climb up there. The walls were smooth and slippery. She clawed at them but she could find no foothold. She called out. Perspiration dripped from her brow and she was overcome with dizziness. She slumped back down to the cold floor of the shaft.

After the initial relief of hearing Aileen's voice there came an overwhelming urgency to do something. Everybody had suggestions to make and Claire still strained to go to her daughter. The foreman crawled forward on his stomach and examined the shaft that had opened up. He saw the child huddled at the bottom.

"Hold on sweetheart," he called softly. "We'll soon have you out of there."

But when he crawled back his face looked grim. "We need to be very careful," he said, "and not do anything foolish. She is at the bottom of a narrow shaft and the ground is very unstable. If we rush in we could cause another rock slide. I think we'd better get a rescue team here."

"Right," said Lambeg, "I'll go and find a phone." He hurried off towards his car, glad to be doing something useful. He felt responsible for what had happened and his whole body was racked with fear and foreboding.

"We can't wait!" cried Claire defiantly. "That shaft could cave in at any moment. It will be ages before he finds a phone and we're miles away from any rescue services. I want her out now."

As if to underline the urgency there came another rattle and cloud of dust from the tunnel. Through it Aileen's voice could be heard calling plaintively. It sounded faint and weak.

"There are bound to be ropes in the back of somebody's van," said Tom Scroggy. "I could go down there and get her out."

"No you couldn't. Your weight would collapse the shaft and anyway you couldn't squeeze down it. It's far too narrow."

"I could do it."

Surprised eyes turned towards Robin Drake.

"I am light enough and I could get down the shaft."

"Robin," said Rosaleen, "Robin, no!" And a look of fear was in her eyes.

"I'll be all right, Mum," said Robin. "It has to be somebody small."

Another ominous growl came from the tunnel. "If I don't go now, it might be too late."

"Are you sure about this?" asked Hugh Bradley holding Robin tightly by the shoulders.

"Yes, I am."

Hugh looked at his daughter and she looked at the pleading face of Claire Scroggy. Then the two women put their arms around each other in silent agreement.

"It just might work," said the foreman. "If there's the slightest danger of the shaft collapsing, we'll pull him out immediately."

Ropes in plenty were found and the stoutest were knotted together and then fastened to a JCB.

"I'll tie one round myself," said Robin, "and take another to tie around Aileen."

"Isn't there a special way of tying the ropes?" asked Hugh anxiously. "Aileen won't be in a fit state to help. She could slip out of the rope."

"I know how to do it, Granda," said Robin. "My dad taught me how to knot ropes for everything."

Very cautiously Robin lowered himself over the side of the shaft. All the men, with Tom Scroggy at their head, were strung along the ropes like a tug of war team. They daren't use the power of the JCB for pulling as the throb of the engine could start another landslide. Inch by inch they let out the rope and Robin descended slowly.

The shaft was very narrow and his face and knees scraped against the side. The bottom widened a little and there was room for him to get down beside Aileen. She was lying slumped in a heap but she was breathing steadily.

"Are you all right, Aileen?" he whispered.

Aileen's eyelids fluttered and opened. A small smile twisted the corners of her mouth. "Chookie-Birdie," she said and her eyes closed again.

Swiftly and expertly Robin looped the rope under Aileen's arms and knotted it securely. Then he gave a tug. Above ground the men began to pull. Robin hoisted Aileen up first and then he came behind her to steady her limp body.

Half way up the earth shuddered again and rubble showered down on them. The rope stopped moving but Robin tugged frantically. The men could see that the whole side of the hill was beginning to move.

"Forget caution now!" shouted Tom. "Pull with all your might!"

Frantically the rope was drawn in and all eyes watched the trembling rocks.

With a frightening roar the hillside collapsed. Screams were heard from the crowd as the rocks tumbled and bounced down the slope. The entrance to the tunnel was completely buried but two dirty, dusty figures were sprawled clear of the rubble.

There were two nurses among the protest group and when they had established that Aileen had no broken bones they decided that it was safe to move her. The Scroggys and the Drakes set off for the nearest hospital which was in Derry and on the way they met Lambeg still desperately looking for a phone.

In the huge hospital Aileen was prodded and X-rayed and wheeled about from one department to another. Faces whirled around her searching and questioning. Finally she was lowered into a lovely warm bath and then tucked into a stiff-sheeted bed. Almost immediately she drifted into a deep sleep. She woke once or twice to see her mother's smiling face and in the morning she was black and blue with bruises and aching with hunger. A check had been kept on her all night and as she only seemed to have suffered a small cut on the head and a mild concussion she was allowed to go home.

∾ A Terrible Discovery ∾

Mrs McCloskey was fed up to the teeth. There had been nothing but interruptions for the past week and she had no peace to get on with preparing for the Spirit of the Foyle Festival and St Patrick's Day was fast approaching. For a start she rarely had a full class. The door opened and there was Mr Quinn. Her heart sank.

"I hope you are not looking for the football team," she said smiling as sweetly as she could. "You had them out for an hour and a half this morning."

"No, not this time," beamed Lambeg and he came into the room and stood swaying on his toes and rubbing his hands. "No, but I'll have them out again tomorrow. We have the best team in all of the Northwest but it takes practice as well as talent to get to the top. And Drumenny will have the cup this year, isn't that right?"

A resounding cheer answered his question. Lambeg looked very pleased with himself. "No it's our other two famous people I'm looking for this time."

The smile froze on Mrs McCloskey's face. "Surely we've had enough of that," she said coldly. "There have been photographers and reporters in and out all week. Isn't it time to let the Grianan incident drop?"

Aileen and Robin had been interviewed many times

since the rescue on Grianan Hill and their photographs had appeared in every local paper and two national papers. Now, most children enjoy a bit of fame and it's nice to have the school notice board full of newspaper articles about your exploits but Aileen and Robin were inclined to agree with Mrs McCloskey. It had not been a happy week for them. Over the past months they had learned to live with the bullying of the Battler Gang and if they kept their heads down it didn't get any worse. Now they were in the limelight and the torture was almost unbearable.

"Oh, it's not the newspapers this time," bellowed Lambeg. "No indeedy. It's Radio Foyle! They've just been on the phone and they want Mr Robin Drake and Miss Aileen Kennedy on the Kate O'Callaghan show tomorrow. Come to my office the pair of you about a quarter to three and we'll make arrangements for getting you there in the morning."

When they came out from Lambeg's office the classroom had emptied and their coats could not be found. Mrs McCloskey stood staring at the rows of empty pegs in the cloakroom and a perplexed frown creased her face.

"Are you sure you had coats with you?" she asked and the uncertainty in her voice underlined the foolishness of the question. It was the coldest day in a bitter week of sub zero temperatures. The children didn't answer.

The bus queue was forming at the door and among the grinning triumphant faces there were a few guilty and unhappy expressions. Aileen and Robin knew that their coats would miraculously reappear tomorrow morning and even the teacher would wonder if she had really witnessed an empty cloakroom.

There was no heat in the bus and Aileen tucked her hands under her arms to try to warm them. Her feet were numb and aching.

"Radio Foyle must be hard up for news," said Wee Willie Clements.

"Yeah," agreed Battler Doherty. "They'll put anybody on to fill up a programme. They had my Auntie May's dog on one time barking to Elvis Presley's 'Hound Dog.'" The gang erupted into a chorus of dog howls while Ronan McCafferty swivelled his hips and played an imaginary guitar. They tired of it after a while and instead began to pass a football up and down the aisle of the bus. Every time they passed Robin they managed to jab him with an elbow or kick him with a heavy-booted foot. Both himself and Aileen got a couple of right hard batters from the ball too before Fonsie McKee, the driver, put an end to the shenanigans.

The cold had now seeped into every bone in Aileen's body and she was thoroughly miserable.

"Are you cold, Scrogs?" Nuala Deery had stuck her head over the seat and was clucking in mock sympathy. "She needs her hero again, Chookie Birdie," she said to a stiff faced Robin. "Can't you see she's foundered?"

"Are you just going to sit there and let her freeze to death?" asked Lisa McCarron joining in the fun. "Go on. Put your arms around her and warm her up."

Aileen stole a quick glance at Robin. He was staring ahead pale and composed but his lips were tinged purple with the cold.

They ran down the rock hard frozen surface of the lane as fast as their numb feet could carry them. They didn't speak; they had nothing to say to each other.

When Robin reached the warmth of the kitchen he was glad to find it empty. He stood shivering in front of the banked-up fire. Warm tears gathered under his closed eyelids and then tumbled on to his frozen cheeks. The latch of the door rattled and lifted. Hastily Robin wiped his face with the sleeve of his jumper.

"That's one would freeze the divil's own furnace," said Hugh Bradley stamping his feet and beating his arms. He stopped when he saw his grandson's woebegone face. "What's up, Robin? Has something happened?"

Robin said nothing. He just went to his room and closed the door quietly behind him. Hugh felt Robin's pain as surely as if he had been slammed in the chest with a sledgehammer.

"We have with us today in the studio two young people who have been hitting the headlines recently and with us also is Ryan Casey, our local expert in archaeology."

Robin and Aileen were sitting paralysed with nerves in the Radio Foyle studio being interviewed by Kate O'Callaghan. Beside them sat a bearded and bespectacled man.

"Aileen," said Kate, "you were inside this tunnel that was discovered on Grianan, indeed you very nearly didn't come out of it again. Was it a very frightening experience?"

"Yes."

"Well, could you tell us what it was like being trapped in there."

"Scary." Aileen pulled nervously at her hair.

"Robin, you were the hero of the hour. Tell us about the dramatic rescue. What did you do?"

"I . . . I . . . I just went down a rope and . . . and . . . got her out."

"I think there's a bit more to the story than that," laughed the exasperated interviewer, "but perhaps we can come back to our shy guests in a moment.

"Ryan, this tunnel under Grianan Hill, what exactly is it?"

To her great relief the archaeologist launched into a flowing account of underground tunnels and what they were used for.

"So, you think that this could be a . . . a . . . a . . . what was it you called it?"

"A *souterrain*."

"Yes, a *souterrain*, what was it you said that was . . . just a place for storing food or for hiding in when the neighbours came to steal the cattle?"

"It could be," smiled the man who loved talking about his subject. "Several such underground tunnels have been discovered around Grianan . . . but . . . "

"Yes?"

"Well, it's impossible to be certain without doing a full scale archaeological dig and that's out of the question at the moment."

"But what else could it be?"

"It could be an ancient tomb."

"How old might it be?"

"Again impossible to say without seeing it. It could date from Neolithic times – that is the New Stone Age – or it could be from the early Christian period. If it was built about the same time as Newgrange tomb in Bru na Boyne near Slane then it would be about five thousand years old and a very important site indeed. If that was the case we would expect to find a long tunnel lined with carved stones and it should open up into a burial chamber. Those tombs were places of ancient worship and of great historical significance. It's a pity Aileen can't describe for us what she saw in the tunnel."

Aileen lowered her eyes and blushed slightly. Amnesia had been a great help any time she had been asked awkward questions.

"Will there be any excavations at all?" asked the interviewer.

"Not in the foreseeable future. I have been out there to do a quick survey and I am certain that any more digging would further damage the site."

"So, there'll be no Heritage Centre?"

"Not at that particular place. They may decide to build well away from the hill itself."

"There's a local legend, isn't there, that inside the Hill of Grianan a band of warriors lies sleeping, awaiting a call to arms?"

Aileen and Robin jerked in surprise and the archaeologist laughed.

"There's a story like that about every ancient site in Ireland. It is of course myth and superstition but an important part of our folklore."

"So, at the moment, the tunnel could be a very important tomb and place of worship – or just a sort of underground larder? We know nothing more about it?"

"Well," said Ryan Casey and then he paused. Kate saw the glint in the archaeologist's eye and her reporter's instincts told her that he had something exciting to reveal.

"You found something at Grianan, didn't you? You know more than you're telling us. Now come on, our listeners want to know everything!"

Ryan Casey laughed.

"You're very persuasive, Kate," he chuckled, "and I suppose now is as good a time as any to make the announcement. We did find something very exciting but as yet we don't know the full significance of the discovery."

"Well tell us," urged Kate O'Callaghan. "Don't keep us in suspense."

"In the middle of the rubble at the caved in entrance to the tunnel we found a large and beautifully carved stone slab. It is superior in quality to anything found at Bru na Boyne and could be indicative of the importance of the site."

"You mean that this must be a Stone Age tomb and not an underground food store. I mean, they didn't go to all the bother of decorating their cupboards, did they?"

"I'm afraid one stone doesn't make a tomb. The slab may have been brought to Grianan from somewhere else or it may have been specially carved for some purpose. At the moment we are just guessing. What is certain is that this stone, we'll call it the Grianan Stone, is one of the finest examples we have at present of the creativity and artistry of the Neolithic period."

"Is it valuable?"

"In terms of adding to our knowledge of the distant past, yes, it could be very valuable."

"What about in money terms – in the oul' pounds and pence. Is it worth a bob or two?"

Ryan Casey squirmed in unease. He did not like putting a monetary value on archaeological artefacts.

"Yes," he admitted grimly. "I'm afraid objects like this have become commodities in the market. If this stone were to be put up for auction internationally, then I am certain it would fetch a frightening price. Our country has been plundered in the past and still is today. Many items are shipped out to fill the pockets of greedy thieves but the Stone of Grianan is safe. Fortunately the people who care about our heritage got there before the pirates."

In the course of his speech Ryan Casey had become agitated and Kate O'Callaghan endeavoured to appease him.

"Yes indeed," she said, "and I'm sure you will take great care of the Grianan Stone. What will happen to it now?"

"Ah," said the archaeologist brightening visibly, "in the past local finds were shipped out to museums in Belfast or Dublin but now we have our own museum and we will be able to keep the Grianan Stone in Derry. First of all, it will be examined by experts who will attempt to establish the possible date of origin and purpose of the stone – believe me this will stir up worldwide interest – it is a very exciting find. Then it will go on view to the public in our new Tower Museum at the O'Doherty Fort in Magazine Street in Derry."

Time was running out and Kate O'Callaghan felt that this was an appropriate point to finish the interview.

"Well, there you have it, folks. If you want to see the Stone of Grianan – which will soon be famous – then go along to the Tower Museum. We will keep you informed about the dates for public viewing. And don't forget – you heard it first on Radio Foyle!"

The signature tune for the ending of the programme filtered through the studio and Kate O'Callaghan removed her earphones and kicked off her shoes.

"That was a good one," she said smiling at Ryan Casey. "You really are excited about this Stone, aren't you?"

"Yes, I am," replied the archaeologist in a whisper; he wasn't quite sure that they were off the air.

The interviewer was already gathering up her papers and thinking about what she would buy in the supermarket on the way home that would be handy for dinner.

"I found something else at Grianan," said Ryan Casey. "You might like to see it." He delved in his pocket and put a tiny object on the table.

"What is it?" asked Kate barely smothering a yawn. She lifted the little figure and surveyed a serenely smiling face. Then she turned it over.

"Ugh!" she said. "It's an ugly wee divil, isn't it? What is it?"

"I'm not quite sure. There are stones called Janus stones with two faces – but they are much bigger and much more crude than this fine little object. Maybe it had some obscure religious significance or it might have been a charm of some sort – you can see there is a little hole there, possibly for stringing around the neck."

"Is it as valuable as the Grianan Stone?"

Ryan frowned as he stuffed the figurine back into his sagging pocket. "It is not as important historically; I don't think we will learn a lot from it. But it is very collectable. It is impossible to put a price on it but I'm sure some unscrupulous collector would pay a lot to have it in his own private museum."

"What will you do with it?"

"It will go on view along with the Grianan Stone," said Ryan Casey as he left the studio.

"Oh!" said Kate when she realised that the children were still sitting there silent and immobile. "You'll find drinks and biscuits outside. Thank you for coming."

The two children sat mute for a few seconds then Aileen spoke in a strangled whisper. "That was the Brod of Bres!" she said. "He has the Brod of Bres in his pocket!"

∞ An Old Familiar Face ∞

"Did you see anything like this?"

The long delicate fingers sifted through the pile of photographs and drawings and then gently nudged one forward for Aileen's attention. She looked at it dully and shrugged.

"Are you sure?"

The soft American accent had hardened a little and Professor Clayton's face twitched with impatience. He had been sitting with Aileen for half an hour now in the headmaster's office trying to get her to describe what she had seen inside Grianan Hill. Illustrations of decorated stone slabs were scattered over the table and pictures of the interior layouts of ancient tombs.

"The Grianan Stone is a very important find, Aileen, and we are anxious to know if there are others like it in the tunnel."

Aileen said nothing.

"You must remember something. It's just a matter of unlocking that memory."

If it wasn't for his accent Aileen would never have guessed that the man was either a professor or an American. He was very ordinary looking in every way. He was dressed in an ordinary grey suit with collar and tie and he had very ordinary features. The only thing extraordinary about him was his voice. It was low pitched and very persuasive. His words were wrapped in a velvety purr that was almost hypnotic so that the listener was lulled and coaxed to talk. He would have made a good psychiatrist.

However, Professor Clayton's golden voice had failed so far to draw Aileen into conversation and he was not pleased. His knuckles whitened as he began to straighten the pictures.

"We'll try once again, shall we?" he said smiling stiffly. "Now just close your eyes and imagine yourself back in that tunnel. Tell me what you see."

To Aileen's great relief the door opened and Lambeg's thundering tones shattered the suffocating peace of the office.

"All finished then?" he rumbled, planting himself firmly in front of the desk. The professor got the message that the headmaster wanted his office back. With a snort of frustration he swept the pictures into his briefcase and left.

Back in the classroom, Aileen slid gratefully into her seat and tried to avoid Mrs McCloskey's disapproving glower. All the poor teacher's hopes that things would soon get back to normal in Drumenny School had been dashed with the discovery of the Grianan Stone. Experts had come from far and wide to visit the Tower Museum and examine the find. It was hailed as the most important artefact ever discovered in the Northwest area and possibly in the whole of Ireland. Professor Clayton was just one of an assortment of investigators who had called at the school to question Aileen. All had gone away defeated.

Because of all the interruptions and the football

practices, the class work for the Spirit of the Foyle Festival was falling further and further behind and this afternoon Mr Quinn was taking the class to Derry to view the now famous Stone.

"Wouldn't you think," said Mrs McCloskey to herself, "he would stay at home after the Grianan debacle?" But Lambeg had no intention of staying at home. The near-disaster at Grianan had been averted and he had put the events of that day completely out of his mind. Now he was glorying in the glare of publicity that surrounded the school.

Robin and Aileen were not so charmed with the outing. Under the teachers' noses the Battler Gang had turned the journey to Derry into a campaign of terror. Aileen's bobbles had been torn from her hair and sent whizzing around the bus and a tin of Coke had "accidentally" been dribbled over her. The short hairs on the back of Robin's neck were viciously and continuously pulled and twisted and a great boot had trampled his crisps into dust. The two children were very relieved when the bus pulled into the bus station and they could escape on to the streets of the city.

"Gosh!" said Robin when he saw the O'Doherty Fort rising majestically above the old city walls. "It must be hundreds of years old."

"About eight or nine," said Aileen.

"Hundred?"

"No, years."

She laughed when she saw the disbelief on Robin's face. He stared at the rough stone of the vertical walls, at the narrow slitted windows and the castellated roof that was ideal for shielding besieged archers.

"You're joking!"

"No, I'm not," replied Aileen. "It's a copy. There used to be a fort there long ago, but that's a copy. Good, isn't it?"

The new Tower Museum was built at the side of the fort and none of the children had ever been in it before. There was an excited buzz when they saw the huge cannon at the entrance that had been salvaged locally from a sunken ship of the Spanish Armada. Near it was an old coach that had featured in the tragic shooting of a beautiful young girl by a man who had come to be known as Halfhanged McNaughton because the rope had snapped during his execution for the murder. Both these items tickled the interest of the children and it was quite some time before the teacher could herd them into the museum proper.

The inside came as a surprise to the children. They had expected to see rows of glass cases with dusty boring exhibits in them but the Tower Museum was an adventure trail. It was tunnelled into the very belly of the old city and as they followed the trail the story of Derry was told by video tapes, narratives, life sized figures in dramatic settings, photographs, posters and plenty of artefacts.

The Grianan Stone was exhibited in the section that told the earliest part of the story. In fact it dominated the other items on display. It was roped off from the pawing hands of curious visitors but otherwise it was unprotected. Lambeg gathered his charges round to admire the Stone and he did so in his usual loud voice so that other visitors to the Museum would know the role Drumenny School had played in the discovery of such an important find.

There wasn't enough room for a class of thirty-five

in the small area reserved for the early times and so some slipped away quietly to explore for themselves. Battler Doherty pushed his way to the front of the remaining children.

"Is that it?" he said in a loud voice. "Did we come all the way in here to see that? Sure it's just a lump of stone with a few scribbles scratched on it. The toilet walls in school have better drawings than that on them."

There were muffled sniggers and giggles around the huddled children but a firm "AHHHEMMM!" from Lambeg soon put a stop to them.

Aileen felt a tingling along her spine and she knew that the Brod of Bres was somewhere close. She peered around and then she saw a small showcase in a recess in the wall. She slid over towards the wall. The case was lit up from within and there, alone and unnoticed, nestled a tiny statue.

There it was – the Brod of Bres! The serenely beautiful face smiled up at her and the ugly, menacing grin was hidden. The little white figurine was so near and yet so far. She could almost feel the slight weight of it around her neck. Tentatively Aileen tried to lift the lid of the glass case. It was locked!

Suddenly her arm was grabbed and she was pulled back into the noisy throng.

"What do you think you're at?" she asked as she shook her arm out of Robin Drake's grip.

"Over there, look!"

"What?" said Aileen looking in the direction indicated. Further along the tunnel a group of people were huddled in conversation. Aileen recognised Ryan Casey and Professor Clayton. They appeared to be answering questions put to them by reporters who were either scribbling in notebooks or holding up tape recorders. She also recognised one of the reporters and her blood froze in her veins.

The girl looked different. She no longer had a punk hairstyle and instead of flashy clothes and dangly earrings she was wearing a baggy jumper, frayed jeans and granny spectacles. But there was no doubt in Aileen's mind who she was. She was the one who had pretended to befriend her and then had led her to the Pit of the Hell Hag where she had been forced to hand the Brod over to the Morrigan. It was Vale Prentess, a servant of the evil Shape-shifter – Vale Prentess, whose name when twisted round spelled SERPENT SLAVE!

"Do you think she's seen us?"

Robin shook his head. "She's too busy being News Person of the Year."

Aileen snorted in disgust.

"She's leaving!" hissed Robin. "Come on. We'll follow her and see where she goes."

"But the teacher and Lambeg . . . "

"We'll not be missed. They'll be here for ages. It'll take hours to go round the whole thing – especially with Lambeg showing off. We'll be back before they've finished."

Vale Prentess was in a hurry. She walked at a brisk pace out through the old gate and into the open space of Guildhall Square. This area of the city was for pedestrians only and fortunately there were plenty of them about. Robin and Aileen, with anorak hoods pulled up against a sudden blast of hailstones, dodged in and out among the strolling shoppers and ornamental trees. Ahead they could see the baggy jumper billowing in the stiff breeze. With head bent Vale hurried on down a narrow street and again the children followed.

Very gingerly, they peeped round the side of a tall building. They were now looking at the back of the Guildhall itself. There was a mushrooming fountain blowing water at passers-by, and a paved area with flower beds and seats for weary shoppers. It was only a short walk from the fountain to the River Foyle but between the two lay a tangle of dual carriageways and roundabouts. Traffic was coming from every direction. Vale was poised at the edge of a footpath and as the children watched she plunged into the traffic flow, weaving and darting between blaring horns and squealing brakes.

"She's going to the river," said Robin. They ran from their hiding place to the paved area and stood up on one of the seats. An icy wind funnelled up from the Foyle and almost tumbled them from their perch. Vale had reached the footpath on the far side of the road and had paused for breath. Then she walked towards the railings that fenced off the river.

Several boats dipped and bobbed in the churning waters. A man was standing on the deck of one. He was too far away for the children to get a good look at him but he was short and broad shouldered with a bulging pot belly. Black hair curled from under a peaked cap. His skin was dark and weather-beaten as if he spent a lot of time in the open. The man helped Vale over the railings and on to the boat. They talked for a few seconds on deck and then disappeared below.

"If we went across there she would see us," said Aileen.

"If we went across there we'd be dead," replied Robin as he eyed the stream of traffic. "I wonder what she's up to?"

"That's easy," replied Aileen. "She's going to steal the Brod and give it to the Morrigan."

"More than likely," agreed Robin. "But what is she doing on that boat?"

There was nothing more the children could find out so they scurried back to the museum and finished the tour.

It was Friday evening and Robin was in the Scroggy house. He and Aileen were sprawled in front of the television laughing at *Neighbours* while Aggie and Claire Scroggy prepared dinner in the kitchen. When the programme was over and the news had come on they switched it off and sat talking.

"I think we should tell my granda and Aggie about today."

"You mean about seeing Vale Prentess?"

"Yes."

Aileen knew that what Robin said made sense. It was Aggie and her uncanny sixth sense, or whatever it was called, who had first suspected Vale Prentess, and it was Aggie and Hugh Bradley who had helped rescue Aileen and recover the Brod. But Aileen felt that the Brod of Bres was her business and at the moment she didn't want to involve anybody else – any mortal that is.

"I think we should tell Mathgen first," she decided.

"And when are we going to tell him?"

"Tomorrow."

❦ The Lucorban ❦

The mountain bikes had been Christmas presents and they were not only their proudest possessions but they were also very useful around the Cloughderg hillside. Robin and Aileen polished them until they glittered and tore around on them any chance they got. Two sturdy helmets had accompanied the bikes and they were compulsory headgear at all times, even if they were only going the short distance between each other's homes.

They were on the road early that Saturday morning and a bitterly cold one it was too. But they were well wrapped up with layers of jumpers under their coats and woolly hats under the helmets. They were going bird watching, they had told their families. Their rucksacks were packed with notebooks and pencils, the *Observer Book of Birds*, loads of grub and of course the powerful binoculars. They probably would take a look at the spectacular early spring comings and goings of the battalions of sea birds around Lough Foyle, but first they were going to find Mathgen.

They stayed on the main road as long as possible but soon they had to go cross country to find Killyshee Wood. The name means the Wood of the Fairy Mound and it was there that one entrance to Mathgen's

Otherworld could be found. They huffed and puffed and strained and went through the gears as they guided the broad tyres over the type of ground that gave the bike its name. Behind them the sun was just tipping Grianan Hill and the sky was a thin watered down blue without a cloud in sight. Later on it would warm up a little but now everything was covered in a white fur of frost and their breath came in pants of dragon smoke.

Killyshee Wood was tucked in a lonely little valley so far off the beaten track that rarely did it see a human visitor. The children themselves had not been back since their last contact with Mathgen some months ago. This was not only because the wood was awkward to get at but also because Mathgen had made it perfectly clear that he would prefer never to see a mortal. Even now the children were not sure how they were going to get in touch with the old Druid. If Mathgen did not want to be contacted then Mathgen would not be contacted.

At the heart of the wood lay a moss-covered boulder beside a dark pool of water. It was the Threshold to Mathgen's world and Robin and Aileen hoped that when they got there they would find a way to make Mathgen cross it in answer to their call. They pushed and pedalled over the rocky terrain hoping that they were going in the right direction. Aileen had been there once, Robin twice, but winter had changed the landscape. The purple sheen of autumn had long gone, the heather was withered and stiffened with frost. Gnarled and naked trees clung to impossible footholds.

A rest was needed. The ground was climbing steadily and they were panting and puffing.

"I thought we should have been there by now,"

wheezed Aileen as she rested her bike against a rock.

"Maybe over the next dip we'll see it," replied Robin uneasily. "I'm starving," he added. Eating would give them time to think. They hoked through the rucksacks until they found the crisps and sat on a rock to replenish their energy. The sun hadn't moved at all in the sky. It still hung suspended behind the hills and, although the sky was cloudless, it seemed to have grown steadily darker – as if it was evening time and not ten o'clock in the morning.

They had worked up a sweat cycling but now that they were resting the cold struck them like a blast from the Arctic. Aileen shivered and crunched her cheese and onion. Robin checked the tyres of the bikes. Then they heard it – the sound that was most dreadful to them. It came softly from behind and then from in front and then from all sides. As the children turned their heads, searching for the vile creature, the squawking grew louder and louder until they had to cover their ears.

Then they saw it – the monstrous evil crow with its grey body and coal-black head and wings. It sat silent now, perched on a rock under a twisted thorny branch, piercing them with its vicious yellow eyes. The black head was thrown back and a long cackle of triumph ripped from the granite beak.

The feathered beast began to shimmer and grow. It shimmered and grew until it stood tall and slender. The body feathers now formed a robe of wispy grey and the wings a gloss-black cloak. Long black hair framed the face, pale and beautiful and deadly. The eyes too had grown larger but they were still yellow and still desperately dangerous. A golden snake curled around the woman's head. It had diamonds for eyes and rubies studded the forked tongue. The same creature decorated the thin black rod that the woman held in a delicate white hand.

"So, we meet again," purred the Morrigan and every word was like a poisoned dart.

"Why are you here?" asked Robin. "We have nothing you would want."

The Morrigan smiled a slow smile and her white teeth gleamed with malice.

Aileen had not spoken. She was too shocked to speak. The appearance of the Morrigan had taken her back to the night she was trapped in her Pit surrounded by the horrible creatures that crawled and squirmed through her Underworld.

"No," said the Morrigan, "you have nothing for me. Soon I will have what I seek. The Brod of Bres will again be mine."

At the mention of the Brod, Aileen shook herself. "You won't get it!" she almost shouted. "We won't let you get it."

An icy ripple of malicious laughter was Aileen's answer.

"And how are you going to stop me? Tell Mathgen that the Brod is once again in danger?" Anger now punctuated the Morrigan's words. "The Children of Danu will not stop me this time. The Fomar will triumph and I will be at their head. With the Brod I will seek the Eye of the exquisite Balor and I will unlock his evil powers. You will not thwart me again. You will not find Mathgen this day. My Lucorban will see to that."

With that the Morrigan raised her black rod and from the serpent eyes a beam flashed and sizzled like forked lightning in an electric storm. The children were blinded by the light and when their vision returned the Morrigan was gone. The air around them was still and seemed to close in on them with a heaviness that sent them into a stupor. A shadow covered the low slung sun so that the light grew dimmer and the hillside seemed to throb and come alive. Before their stupefied eyes the ground became pock-marked with gaps and holes. Creatures began to crawl from the fissures and soon the hillside was carpeted with a seething swarm that shifted and shunted in a terrifying rattle.

The things were as big as satellite dishes and looked like overgrown cockroaches. Polished brown armour plating covered bloated pink bellies that were revealed when the creatures stood upright. The heads were small compared with the gross bodies and the faces had features that were almost human. The monsters possessed many short thick hairy legs and one long one which ended in a vicious crab-like pincer. The ugly giant insects advanced towards the terrified children.

"What are they?" screamed Aileen as she drew her legs up underneath her body.

"Well, they're not ladybirds anyway," answered a frightened Robin. "We have to get out of here."

They began to scramble down the slope but behind them they could hear the growing clatter as the monstrous army advanced on legs and claws.

"They're catching us!" screamed Aileen.

"Pelt them!" shouted Robin and he was hurling stones and screaming at the top of his voice and with the ferocity of a trapped tiger. Aileen scooped up a handful of the sharp stones that littered the ground and she too launched into battle.

The creatures were now within feet of the children and Aileen's stomach heaved as the ugly heads pushed towards her. Black eyes bulged above bulbous noses and yellow tusks of teeth hung over thick purple lips. Pincers waved excitedly in the air and their saw edges snapped open and shut in greedy anticipation. Those to the front were struck by the hail of stones on their soft bellies and, whimpering like babies, they cowered behind rocks for protection. But they were swept mercilessly aside with a sickening crunch as others came tumbling down the hill. A wall of pincers surrounded the children and there was no escape from the repulsive ranks. Soon they would be crushed by the menacing claws and shredded by the yellow tusks!

A pincer reached out and snapped close to Aileen's ankle as if the horrible creature wanted to tease her as a cat plays with a mouse. She screamed, closed her eyes tightly and held her breath. She felt Robin's arm around her shoulder and it was shaking. She waited in terror. Nothing happened. Then came a tremendous uproar of clattering and crunching that made her open her eyes.

The creatures were still there but they were tumbling over each other to escape back down the holes they had crawled from! At first Aileen could see no reason for the panicked flight but then she saw that some of the claws were sealed with skeins of sticky thread. Through the air, from every direction, more threads criss-crossed to entwine the deadly pincers rendering them useless.

"Look!" crowed Robin in delight. And Aileen looked. The hillside was dotted with people no taller than the children themselves; people whom the children knew and loved. It was the Annalaire, the people of the air who were friends of Mathgen and the Danu and who had helped Robin and Aileen before.

"There's Cathara," she shouted gleefully, "and Allochar!"

The tiny twins stood atop a boulder and a look of deep concentration furrowed their delicate faces. Their arms were outstretched and hands extended. Every finger spun a silken thread that flew with breathtaking speed towards the fleeing monsters. Similar threads flew from many pairs of Annalaire hands.

Breathlessly Robin and Aileen watched as pincers were bound and trussed and owners crashed into each other in great heaps like a grisly traffic pile-up. The Annalaire now jumped down from their perches and chased their victims who reared up menacingly and flapped useless claws. Reed blowpipes were raised to pursed lips and mouthfuls of pin-like darts showered into exposed soft underbellies. The monsters howled and yelped and scuttled away into crevices and shadowed creases in the hillside. In a few minutes not a trace of them was left.

"What have you done to call the Lucorban from their holes in the earth?" inquired Cathara and her beautiful violet eyes were worried.

"We didn't call them, Cathara," answered Aileen. "It was the Morrigan."

Allochar now stood beside his sister. Brother and sister were identical in looks but for the feathery red-gold beard that fringed Allochar's chin. They were dressed in the dreamy colours of dawn and both had bulging pouched bags strapped to waists and across shoulders. In these pouches the Annalaire kept their secrets, for they were the people who breathed life into

61

sleeping winter trees and filled the flowers with dewy nectar.

"The Morrigan? But what did she want with you?"

"She was trying to keep us from bringing some news to Mathgen," answered Robin.

"Bad news?"

The children nodded.

Allochar sighed. "When mortals come it is always bad news."

Then the twins shook hands formally with Robin and Aileen and the children enquired politely after the health of the twins and their people.

"Dreadful," complained Allochar. "We are creatures of the air and the mortals are filling it with poisons and pestilence. Soon the Annalaire will die of suffocation." He coughed a hollow cough to prove his point.

"Oh, he's just an old moaner," laughed Cathara. "There is truth in what he says but we have survived a lot and we will learn to live with our present problems." She shook her long golden tresses at her grumpy brother.

"There lies the Wood of the Threshold," said Allochar ignoring her. "We will take you to Mathgen." To the children's great surprise they saw that the lie of the land was now familiar to them. The black shadow had lifted from the sun, which was now higher in the sky, and the little wood of Killyshee lay only a few feet away.

"Why could we not see it before?" asked a puzzled Aileen.

"That was the work of the Morrigan," explained Cathara. "She can hide the familiar with her cloak of confusion. She brought the darkness on the earth because her Lucorban are creatures who love the dark and are loath to come into the daylight."

"Our bikes are up the hill a bit," said Robin. "We'll get them and meet you at the wood."

The twins sent the rest of the Annalaire down into the wood but they didn't go themselves. They were curious about these bikes. So Robin and Aileen had to show them how they worked and their friends' eyes grew wide with wonder as they saw the children on the funny machines. Nothing would do them but they would have a go. They fell off a few times and Robin feared that the two prized possessions would end up wrapped in sticky thread from frustrated fingers, but they soon got the hang of it and went hurtling down the hill to the wood, whooping with pleasure.

"Could you credit that?" asked a bemused Aileen. "They can move through the air with the speed of a jet-propelled bumblebee but look at the pleasure they're getting from a couple of bikes."

When the children reached the wood, Cathara was covered in a tumble of dried leaves and moss and anxiously, Aileen examined her bike for damage. But all was in order and Cathara didn't seem any the worse for her daring adventure.

"Will Mathgen see us do you think?"

Allochar shrugged. "Who knows what Mathgen will do? We can only try."

Robin and Aileen followed the twins into the centre of the wood. Dead leaves, stiff with cold, crunched under foot and the pale sun barely penetrated the tangle of bare branches. The large boulder stood shrouded in moss and the water in the pool was black and still. Cathara and Allochar placed their hands on the rock and began to chant in a language that the children did not understand. At first nothing happened then the rock began to tremble and pulsate with a white light that grew in intensity until the children were blinded.

From the heart of the light the children heard a familiar voice.

"What is it this time? Why have I been called once again across the Threshold?"

The light dimmed and then disappeared. In front of the rock stood the magnificent figure of Mathgen. Tall and erect he stood with his silver hair and beard flowing freely over broad shoulders. His body was wrapped in a robe of open-weave cloth the colour of butter and around him billowed a cloak, green as a new spring leaf. Gaudy designs of fabulous animals curled and laced around the edges of the cloak rearing their heads in grotesque and fanciful poses. In his wizened hand the old druid held his white rod of power.

"We have brought the mortals again," said Allochar. He looked Mathgen straight in the eye but there was a trace of wariness in his voice. The Annalaire were not of the Danu people and Mathgen was not their Chief Druid but they depended on Mathgen's High Magic to protect them from the Morrigan and her evil slaves.

"For a thousand circles of the sun my peace in the Otherworld has been undisturbed, but now I am back and forward across the Threshold like a darting swallow," grumbled the Druid. Robin looked at Aileen. It was months since Mathgen had last been summoned across the Threshold.

"Time must fly in the Otherworld," he whispered to Aileen.

"What was that?" The old Druid seemed to see the children for the first time and he sighed a sigh that came from the soles of his sturdy sandals. "Robin of the Questions and Aileen the Fair! I fear the worst. What disasters do you carry with you today?"

"It is the Brod again," said Aileen.

"The Brod? The Brod of Bres? But what have you to tell me about that I don't already know? It lies safe with the slumbering Warriors of the goddess Danu."

"No it doesn't," said Robin. "It is in a museum in Derry in a glass case. It's there for the whole world to see."

"Nonsense!" fumed the Druid. "Wasn't it myself who rescued it from the Morrigan and so saved all the Worlds from her evil designs? Isn't it myself who is the Guardian of the Brod and didn't I place it under the protection of the Warriors myself?"

Aileen giggled but stopped when Mathgen threw her a fierce look from under his bushy eyebrows. She didn't dare remind the Druid that his High Magic had not worked on that fearful night in the Morrigan's den and that the Brod had been rescued by mortals and Annalaire and then sent to Grianan by the goddess Danu.

Robin told Mathgen what had happened at the Grianan of Aileach but still the Druid was loath to accept that the Brod of Bres was once again threatening the peace of the Children of Danu. Aileen had come prepared for this; she knew that the Druid would be hard to convince. She reached into her rucksack and produced a *Derry Journal*.

"What is this?" asked Mathgen as he held the paper between finger and thumb. "What squigglings and squirmings do you show me?" he asked disdainfully.

"There!" said Aileen pointing at a photograph. "What do you think that is?"

Mathgen gasped and clutched the paper in both hands. 'HISTORIC FINDS!' blared the headline and a photograph of the great Stone of Grianan occupied most of the front page. But underneath it was a smaller photo. It was unmistakably the Brod of Bres.

"What magic is this?" screamed the Druid flapping the newspaper in horror. "Is this the work of the Morrigan?"

"No," replied Aileen. "That's a bit of mortal magic. But now you see that the Brod isn't safe with the warriors and the Morrigan is after it again. Vale Prentess knows where it is and the Morrigan tried to stop us coming to tell you. She would have succeeded too if the Annalaire hadn't turned up."

"Is this true?" Mathgen had addressed his question to Cathara and Allochar. They nodded.

"Yes," said Cathara. "The Morrigan had unleashed the Lucorban."

"The Lucorban! She dared to call forth those beasts of the dark!"

"You know the Lucorban, then?" asked Robin.

"Those Fomar monsters have waged war on the Danu in the past and will do so again if the Morrigan can claim the Brod and the power that it will unlock."

"Do you think," Robin asked Aileen in a whisper, "that these Lucorban could be anything to the Leprechauns in your fairy stories?"

Aileen shuddered remembering the snapping claws and dripping tusks.

"I hope not!" she said. "I wouldn't want them living at the bottom of my garden."

Mathgen had begun pacing up and down in the small clearing in the woods. Every so often he would stop and mutter angrily under his breath. Aileen cleared her throat to remind him that they were still there.

"Shush!" hissed the old man. "I am thinking!"

On and on he paced and muttered. Robin coughed politely. Mathgen glared at him.

"It takes time to think," he said.

"What are you going to do?" Robin asked impatiently.

"There you go again, Robin of the Questions! I will retrieve the Brod, of course, and return it to the Warriors. That's what I will do."

"Aren't the warriors under a ton of rubble?" asked Aileen.

"Of course not! Only the tunnel is closed. The warriors of Danu still slumber in their chamber. They can never die." By now Mathgen was really exasperated.

"But how will you get the Brod out of the museum?" asked Robin.

"With my High Magic of course!"

"Will it be strong enough to get the Brod and stop the Morrigan? Have you got a plan?"

This time it was Aileen who had spoken. Mathgen was affronted that she dared to doubt his powers.

"My Magic is my business and I would thank you to mind yours," he said in his haughtiest tone. "I, Mathgen, Chief Druid to the Kings and Queens of the Danu, am more than a match for the Morrigan and her base Magic. I will have a plan and it will be stupendous."

He handed the *Journal* back to Aileen and added, "I thank you for bringing me this warning. Now you may go and rest easy, the problem is safe in my hands. I, Mathgen, will once again rescue the Brod of Bres."

The children went home but their minds did not rest easy. They had no great confidence in Mathgen and his stupendous plans. Worry gnawed at Aileen as she thought of the little statue and the perils it could bring.

∾ Boredom ∾

Robin Drake was just not interested in the preparations for the Spirit of the Foyle Festival. Almost all of the time in school was taken up with it now. The class had to present a scene showing "A Day in the Life of a Stone Age Village" and whenever the football team wasn't outside practising, a frenzy of rehearsals was going on in the classroom. The children were divided into working groups each with a particular task to do. Some would be making axes, spears and arrows and others would be fashioning stone implements for ploughing or reaping. One group scraped skins with stone tools whilst others ground wheat ears between two large stones. There were spinners and weavers, potters and farmers, bakers and shoemakers.

Whole sheep and goat skins and bags of raw wool had been scrounged from every possible source. Parents helped to twist and spin the wool into mountains of dirty grey skeins. Aggie Scroggy washed the wool until it was creamy white and then she gathered lichens and seaweed and collected onion skins from every household. These she brewed in huge cauldrons and then some of the skeins of spun wool were dipped into the different pots. They dried into pale greens and greys, and soft yellows and browns. Most of the community had volunteered to help and almost every home was a hive of very ancient industry. One old man still had a loom in an outhouse and he happily wove the wool into handy lengths.

"It's all a bit stupid, isn't it?" said Robin as he surveyed the Scroggy kitchen. The cauldrons were bubbling on the cooker, a smell of wet wool seeped through the room.

"What is?" asked Aileen

"All this history stuff."

Aileen didn't look up. She was busily twirling a home-made spindle. She liked the feel of the oily wool as it slipped through her fingers and she had discovered that she was very good at spinning. A mound of spun wool was growing at her feet.

"I dunno," she said. "I'm enjoying it really, and there's nothing else to do in this weather."

A steady stream of rain poured down outside and the kitchen window was steamed up with the boiling of pots. Robin felt restless.

"Will I go and get my Monopoly game?" he asked.

"I'm not in the mood," replied Aileen, again without lifting her head. "And besides, I have to get through all that lot today." She indicated a heap of unspun wool that sat in fat rolls, like white sausages, waiting for her attention.

"Well, I'll see you then," said Robin rising to go. Aileen nodded but she didn't seem to notice that he was leaving.

Back in his own house things weren't much better. His mother was stitching up strips of woven material into knee-length tunics and his grandfather was working in his shed. Robin could hear the steady clink of metal on metal and he knew that his grandfather had abandoned his usual tinkering with electronics and was working on the dug-out canoe. This would be used in the flotilla of "Boats Through the Ages" that would sail up the Foyle at the climax of the celebrations.

Boredom grew on Robin like mould on stale bread. All this song and dance about the pageant was a mystery to him. He knew nothing about the history of the Foyle and he didn't want to know anything. He didn't feel part of the preparations. Even Aileen was shutting him out. Every time he called for her she was working with that stupid old spindle.

"You didn't stay long," said his mother looking up from her sewing. "Was Aileen not in?"

"She's busy."

Robin poured himself a drink and then went to his room. Rosaleen sighed and went back to her work.

In his room Robin flung himself on his bed and reached under it for his special box. It was now almost full of neatly filed letters from his father. He emptied the box on to the bed and spread the letters out. Slowly he read through each one as he had done at least a couple of times a week since they had started arriving. He laughed again at the jokes he had laughed at a dozen times before. He read too the questions that he never answered when he was writing back.

Every letter asked about football, even the one he had received that day:

"You still haven't told me about the school football team. I bet you're really showing them a thing or two. How many goals have you scored this season?"

Carefully Robin folded the letters and placed them back in the box. He lay back on the bed and looked at the ceiling. How could he begin to tell his dad what it was like in Drumenny School? He missed his old school in Manchester. He had been happy there and even though his dad wasn't living with them they saw a lot of each other. And best of all was the football. He looked over at the big cardboard box beside the wardrobe – the box that held all his football stuff. Then he got up off the bed.

A loud thud at the shed door almost caused Hugh Bradley to miss the chisel and hit his thumb. He went to look out the window. There was a flat grassy area between the shed and the house and Robin was out there. The rain had stopped and he was dribbling a football swiftly and skilfully along the ground. Every so often he would slam it against the door of the shed' with such force that the ball shot back like a bullet. His grandfather was mesmerised by the speed and grace of the dancing feet as Robin bobbed and dodged, avoiding imaginary defenders. Rosaleen had told him about Robin's talent but this was the first time he had ever seen the boy kick a ball

As he moved swiftly and elegantly over the ground, Hugh could see that Robin's lips were moving. He was talking to himself in his lonely battle against an invisible team of giants. His face was full of anger. Hugh was saddened by the terrible waste of talent. The thudding went on until it began to grow dark. Then Robin went inside and put his football back in the box.

❦ A Robbery ❦

The radio was murmuring away in the background and Robin was just about to take his first delicious bite of a bacon sandwich when the words of the news reader stopped him dead.

" . . . the thieves entered the museum some time over the weekend and stole the Stone that had been found recently at the Grianan of Aileach. There appears to be no sign of a break-in and police are questioning all who had access to keys. Experts say that the Grianan Stone could be worth a very large sum on the black market and they are anxious to trace it before it leaves the country. A small two-faced statue was also taken from a glass case during the robbery . . . "

The reader's voice trailed on but Robin was no longer listening. He left the rest of his sandwich and jumped up from the table. Hurriedly he packed his bag with school books and then he went into his bedroom and took the five-pound note that had been in the last letter from his father. Back in the kitchen his mother was wrapping up his lunch.

"What's up with you?" asked Rosaleen Drake. "It's not like you to be so quick off the mark on a Monday morning."

He waited where the lane forked but it seemed ages

before Aileen appeared.

"Did you hear?" he asked as soon as he saw her grumpy Monday face.

"What?"

"The news?"

"I never listen to the news."

"The Stone's gone and so's the Brod!"

Aileen tried to shake the sleep from her drowsy brain as Robin told her what he had heard on the radio.

"Was it Mathgen, do you think? He said he would get it back."

"But he wouldn't take the Stone, would he?" replied Robin.

"No," agreed Aileen. "It has to be Vale Prentess then. But she's only interested in the Brod too."

"Maybe," nodded Robin. "Maybe she's greedy. She steals the Brod for the Morrigan for what she can get out of her and she steals the Stone for somebody else who is willing to pay a lot of money. She's sort of hedging her bets."

"Or killing two birds with one Stone?"

Robin groaned and punched her playfully.

"We must be serious," said Aileen straightening her face. "We have to find out who took the Brod and we have to find out today."

Robin had guessed that Aileen would say exactly that.

"Well, I've got a plan," he announced importantly.

"You have?" said Aileen and her eyes widened.

"Yes. We'll dump our bags in the hedge and hide when the school bus comes. Then, ten minutes later, we'll get on the service bus to Derry and go into town and see what we can find out."

"You mean dob school?"

"If that means the same as mitching – then, yes."

"I have no money for the bus, the school pass won't work."

Robin waved his five-pound note under her nose and Aileen smiled in admiration. She was more than willing to go along with his plan and Robin was glad of the excuse to avoid another day steeped in "A Day in the Life of a Stone Age Village."

They stuck their bags well in under a bush and hid in the lane as the bus stopped. The driver waited for a while in case the children had overslept and then he took off again. Half an hour later they kept their heads down as they passed by the school in the service bus.

"There's one thing we didn't think about," said Aileen as they rolled along the empty road. "Vale Prentess couldn't lift that stone. It's far too heavy. She'd have needed help."

"There's that man she met on the boat," suggested Robin. "He had arms like a wrestler's."

Aileen nodded. "Yes," she said. "But I don't think even the two of them could shift it."

Guildhall Square was almost empty of casual shoppers but two British army jeeps were parked under the walls. Soldiers stood at the corners of every building lining the square.

"Did your dad patrol like that?" asked Aileen.

"I suppose he did. He was only here for one tour. He was never sent back after he married my mum."

"Did you stay with him in an army barracks when you were over after Christmas?"

"No," laughed Robin. "I stayed in my gran's house but my dad was there on leave."

"You have a granny in England?"

"Yes. And another granddad. In Manchester. And I have uncles and aunts and cousins there too."

Aileen was surprised. She thought that when Robin's mother came back home only Robin's father had been left behind in England but he had a whole family over there. She looked at the soldiers again. Most times she never even noticed them though they were always on the streets and the country roads. They were just moving uniforms without faces. But maybe one of them lived beside Robin's granny in Manchester?

"What do you feel like when you see the soldiers?"

Robin looked at her and Aileen could see him struggling to answer the question.

"All mixed up," he said finally and Aileen nodded.

"Yes," she agreed. "I've lived here all my life and I don't understand any of it."

The broad span of the old gate was cordoned off with white tape and a small crowd had gathered round. The children could see through the arch to the door of the museum and a little knot of people was standing on the steps. There were policemen in flak jackets and reporters with notebooks. Aileen could see Professor Clayton looking as ordinary as ever and Ryan Casey with his hair standing on end and looking as if he hadn't slept in a month. One of the reporters was Vale Prentess.

"She's still here then," whispered Aileen. "She hasn't cleared off yet."

"She has to stick around for a while," said Robin, "so as not to look suspicious." The girl stood scribbling in her notebook and then she zipped up her waxed jacket against the wet cold and left. Robin and Aileen were not far behind her.

It was easy at first to follow Vale Prentess. She left Guildhall Square and walked along the Strand Road which is one of the main shopping centres. There were some shoppers around by this time and the children managed to hide behind bodies or dodge into shop doorways. If Vale got one glimpse of them they would be recognised and then they would have no hope of ever finding the Brod of Bres.

The girl turned into a street that climbed steeply away from the river. This was a street of tall terraced houses lined with leafless trees. They had to risk being seen but they hoped that if Vale did turn round the slender trunks of the trees would hide them.

Half way up the hill the girl turned right, into another street. Now that she was out of sight they could race openly up the hill in hot pursuit. They stopped to catch their breath and to take a cautious peek round the corner. Another tree provided cover and they were now looking along a broad, level street. Facing the children was a tall red-brick house covered from chimney to doorstep in the skeleton vines of a creeping plant. It was the last house in an elegant old terrace and Vale Prentess was turning a key in the front door.

"What do we do now?" asked Robin. "If we come out into the open we will be in full view from the house."

Aileen thought for a while. "There is a lane at the side of the house," she said.

"I see it."

"It must go up behind all the houses and out at the top. If we go on up this street we might find the top entrance to the back lane."

"I think you could be right," agreed Robin. And sure enough when the children had run up the hill to where the street stopped at a main road and then along the footpath they found the next street and the back lane. The lane was dark and overhung with dripping branches. They crept down past closed back gates until they came to the bottom gate.

"Now what?" asked Aileen.

The bottom house had a garden to the side that was closed off from the lane by a slatted wooden fence.

"Look there," said Robin. A section of the fence had gaps in it where slats had been broken and not replaced. "Do you think we could squeeze in there?"

They could and they did. They crept along the wet grass until they were tucked under the sill of a long narrow window. Inside they could hear a telephone ringing. Someone picked it up. The phone was beside the window and just above their heads was an ornate wrought iron grille – a decorative air vent. Their astonished ears could hear every word that was spoken.

"That's more than we agreed," came the flat-toned voice of Vale Prentess. "You're going back on your word." The girl then listened for a while and when she spoke again her voice was angry.

"I know it's risky. It's risky for all of us . . . "

There was silence again and then frustration coloured the girl's voice.

"OK! OK! I'll get you the money tomorrow but you'd better have a good plan, otherwise we'll find some other way . . . "

Again there was a listening pause.

"Right," said Vale and she now sounded decisive.

"I'll meet you at half four tomorrow – at Lloyd's Bank."

The phone was slammed back on the receiver. The children scuttled out through the hole in the fence and didn't stop running until they were back in the city centre and looking for a café to have a warm cup of tea.

Aileen licked the cream that oozed out through the side of her doughnut and thought that sitting in the nice warm café was certainly better than school.

"What did you make of that?" asked Robin as he sucked the sugar off his fingers.

"Well, I think she was talking to the man from the boat about a plan to smuggle the Grianan Stone out of the country. That means she has the Brod too."

"Mm," agreed Robin. "I wonder what she's going to do with it?"

"She's going to give it to the Morrigan of course!"

"Maybe and maybe not. Maybe the Morrigan thinks that is what will happen. But you heard what Ryan Casey said about the Brod fetching a big price. She didn't do too well last time she helped the Morrigan, did she? Could be she's going to sell the Stone and the Brod too."

A piece of doughnut stuck in Aileen's throat causing her to choke.

"She wouldn't dare!" she spluttered. "She knows what the Morrigan would do to her if she tried!"

"Yes, I suppose you're right," nodded Robin. "But there's something else too."

"What?"

"There's more than two of them."

"How do you work that out?"

"Well, when Vale Prentess was on the phone she

said, 'It's risky for all of us,' not both of us. And, the museum wasn't broken into. So there has to be somebody who knew where the keys were kept."

Aileen was impressed by Robin's detective work.

"You're right," she said. "But who could it be?"

"Ah," smiled Robin. "Now there is a mystery. We might find out more tomorrow. She's arranged to meet somebody at the bank – probably the man from the boat so that she can pay him – and we'll be there too."

"But we couldn't be in Derry for half four tomorrow unless we dobbed school again!"

"Maybe that's what we'll have to do," said Robin. "But right now we'd better get to the bus station or we'll miss the bus back to Cloughderg."

The service bus left them at the top of the lane only ten minutes later than the school bus but they hurried home and nobody noticed the difference at all. After dinner Robin and Aileen took the yellow pages of the phone book up to Aileen's room and sat poring over it looking for Lloyd's Bank. To their great disappointment they couldn't find it.

"It must be here somewhere," said Robin.

"Well, it isn't," replied Aileen. "There isn't a Lloyd's Bank in Derry nor anywhere in the whole district so what are we going to do now?"

There was nothing they could do. Reluctantly Robin went home to ponder and puzzle the mystery well into the night and Aileen sat staring out her window into the darkness. Aggie Scroggy found her there when she was going to bed and saw the light still on.

"Are you not asleep yet, Aileen?" she asked. "Is there something disturbing you?"

Aileen could see that Aggie knew the Brod had been

stolen and that Aileen was worried about it. But the old woman would not talk about it unless Aileen introduced the subject first.

"I just can't sleep," she replied.

Aggie said goodnight and was about to leave the room when Aileen asked, "Aggie, did there used to be a Lloyd's Bank anywhere in Derry?"

Aggie looked puzzled.

"Lloyd's Bank?" she said almost to herself and began to shake her head. "There's a lot of banks but I don't remember any Lloyd's Bank." Then her brow cleared and she smiled. "No, there isn't one in Derry," she said. "But there's one right here in Cloughderg."

"A bank in Cloughderg!" said Aileen in astonished disbelief. "Sure there isn't even a shop here."

"It isn't a building for hoarding money," smiled Aggie. "It's a bank of the river. On the other side of the hill, where you were the other day with the sheep, the land falls steeply to the side of the Lough. There is a little inlet there called Lloyd's Bank. An old man of that name, old Matthew Lloyd, used to live there long ago. There's nothing there now. I'm sure a living creature hasn't been down to Lloyd's Bank in many's a year."

"Could you get to it by car?" asked Aileen trying to smother her excitement.

"Not right down to it. But there is a track of sorts from the main road and it's not a very long walk." Aggie was looking troubled again. She stood for a moment waiting for Aileen to tell her why she wanted to know about the lonely inlet that nobody ever visited. But Aileen said nothing.

"Whatever you're thinking about, Aileen – take care," she said and left the girl to mull over this new bit of information. Vale Prentess would know about Lloyd's Bank, she told herself, for the girl had travelled round Cloughderg a lot when she was last here. But who was she arranging to meet there and why so far out in the wilds?

∞ An Unplanned Boat Trip ∞

"It is very strange that you were both sick yesterday," said Mrs McCloskey in her "I don't believe one word you are saying" voice. "You know the school rule, you have to bring a note when you have been absent. I will have to inform Mr Quinn and he will get in touch with your . . . "

Fortunately for Robin and Aileen there was now a timely interruption that took all of Mrs McCloskey's attention and let them off the hook. It was not so fortunate for Wee Willie Clements.

Ronan McClafferty came hurtling into the classroom wearing his football strip. "Mr Quinn says you're to come quick!" he panted and his face was pale. "Willie Clements is hurt bad!"

Out on the football pitch Wee Willie was on the ground writhing in pain and his left leg lay limp and twisted at an awkward angle. Lambeg was crouched down beside him and the rest of the players were huddled in small groups, flapping arms or jumping up and down to keep warm.

Poor Willie had a broken ankle. His parents were fetched and he was carted off to the casualty department in the hospital in Derry. There were a lot of long faces in the school that day and longest of all was

Lambeg's. Everybody was sorry for Willie of course but the bitterest blow of all was the loss of the striker on the Drumenny team. The cup final was only days away and without Willie the school didn't stand a chance. Lambeg spent the rest of the day trying out hopefuls but the talent displayed did not bring a smile to his face.

Mrs McCloskey tried to get the class to rehearse for the pageant but nobody could raise much enthusiasm. A cloud of depression had come to rest over the sloped roof of Drumenny School. Aileen and Robin, however, were thinking of other things. Robin had tossed and turned all night wondering what they were going to do in the morning and had done a victory dance when Aileen told him that Lloyd's Bank was right beneath their noses. They would have plenty of time after school to get there before half past four.

Once home they both grabbed something to eat then rushed out again leaving their mothers standing shaking their heads and wondering what prank they were up to now. It was just four but they wanted to be in place before Vale Prentess showed up. Aggie Scroggy went to the door and stood looking after the fleeing bodies as they leapt and raced up the field. She had no doubt where they were going.

Once over the hill the children slowed down and began to creep stealthily forward. Before them lay the great expanse of Lough Foyle. Down towards the water the slope was a tangle of willow and blackthorn bushes. Velvet buds tipped the willows but the thorns tore at their faces and clothes. Small trees hung dangerously over the waters, their roots embedded in a thin layer of soil and their gnarled branches screening the little inlet from the eyes of the world. The waters of the lough lapped gently against a rocky shore that was fringed with a narrow strip of pebbles. It was dark and sheltered in the little cove and in the calm and unruffled waters a half-decker boat bobbed and swayed.

"It's the same boat!" breathed Aileen in a hoarse whisper. "That's why the meeting is out here. A boat could stay hidden there forever and nobody would see it. Maybe the mysterious third man, or person, will be on board."

As she spoke a peaked cap appeared from below deck and a figure stretched his brawny arms and looked towards an overgrown track that led towards the main road.

"It's him," said Robin. "The man she was talking to in Derry." Then he too looked at his watch. It was now nearly a quarter to five and it was growing dark. They tried to make themselves comfortable in their little hollow and settled down to wait and watch.

"It's well after five," whispered Aileen. "Maybe she's not coming?"

The man on the boat too had grown impatient. He had smoked cigarette after cigarette flicking his butts over the side of the boat so that the calm water was littered with cork tips.

Just then the engine of a car coughed and died up on the main road. Someone was coming! Would Vale Prentess be alone or would she bring her mysterious partner? Would the children see who was prepared to steal the Grianan Stone and pay to have it smuggled out of the country?

The girl was unaccompanied. She came down the path, almost smothered in dead ferns and thorny branches, and climbed on board the boat. The voices travelled over the water so that the children had no difficulty hearing the conversation.

"What kept you? I thought you weren't coming," said the man gruffly.

"There was a checkpoint on the road," answered the girl. "They took the car apart."

"Well, what's the story?"

"We've agreed to pay the price you're asking – if you come up with a foolproof plan. Right now it's too dangerous to move the Stone at all. But we must get it away soon."

"I have a plan," answered the man and he sounded pleased with himself. "It's a very simple plan. We just sling that oul' over-rated gravestone on board and take off right under their noses."

"That's not a plan," said the girl angrily. "That's just stupid talk. There are checkpoints on every road out of Derry so we couldn't bring it out here. The quays are crawling with patrols and army boats are up and down the river all the time so if you brought the boat into the city we still couldn't bring the stone on board without being seen."

"We could – if we do it my way," said the man slowly and deliberately.

"And what's your way?" asked Vale Prentess.

To the despair of the children the man then said, "It's cold up here. Why don't we go below and I can tell you over a cup of tea."

The cabin door swung closed behind them and not a word of the conversation could the children hear.

"If we moved out on to that rock there," said Robin, "we could step on to that ledge."

Aileen looked thoughtfully at the boat. It was a fair size and there was a raised platform that ran right round the cabin area. There wasn't much cover and it was very risky.

"You're on," she whispered.

They stepped quietly over the rail of the boat on to the ledge and then crouched down by the side of the cabin window. They could hear voices now but not as clearly as before. The conversation came in snatches over the sound of running water and clanking crockery.

" . . . you mean right there . . . out in the open . . . ?"

" . . . best way . . . place bunged up with all that traffic . . . who would notice?"

" . . . could work . . . crowds and noise . . . move quickly . . . not much time . . . "

There was a clink of delph being dumped into a sink and the boat swayed with rapid movement. Robin and Aileen decided it was time to abandon ship and jump back on to their rock. To their horror they discovered that the boat had drifted away from the rock leaving a gap too wide to jump. The door of the cabin opened and when the boatman saw what had happened he started the engine and took the boat back towards the shore to allow Vale Prentess to climb off. But the children were trapped! They were huddled down on the other side of the cabin and if they moved at all they would be seen.

As Vale Prentess stepped ashore a noisy flapping of wings broke the silence of the evening. The girl stopped still and clutched her anorak close against her throat. A huge grey crow descended out of nowhere and settled on the branch of a tree above her trembling head. They stared at each other, the girl and the bird, for a few silent seconds. Vale shivered and in the fast fading light her face looked pale as death. The bird squawked a warning threat but the girl stood her ground. She covered her eyes with a shaking hand, breaking the hypnotic glare of the baleful yellow eyes. Then the ugly beak opened wide and screamed a long and evil curse into the purple evening. With her eyes still covered Vale ran in panic through the undergrowth. The crow sat still as a statue, its yellow eyes unblinking. Then it rose smoothly and sailed off over the trees and rocks into the unknown.

The man moved about on deck with the engine ticking over and the children remained huddled in their small space at the side of the cabin. If only he would go below, even for a minute, they could slip over the side and be off.

But the man didn't go below. Instead he began to move off. The boat chugged slowly up the Lough hugging the bank and the cover that the overhanging trees gave. It was now dark and it was gloomy under the tunnel of trees. They were so close to the shore that branches brushed against the children's faces as they passed by. So close and yet so far away!

All sorts of thoughts crowded the children's frightened minds. Where were they going and what would happen to them when the man finally found them?

ᖇᖇ Football Fury ᖇᖇ

A loud oath ripped through the cold gloom and the engine was slammed into reverse. The boat came to a halt so suddenly that the children slid forward and were almost thrown out under the rail. This is it, they thought, he has seen us. Robin risked a quick peek and he realised that the man was not looking at them at all. He was staring straight over their heads out into the darkness. Robin followed the man's gaze. Then he nudged Aileen.

Up ahead of the boat a filmy white shape was floating just above the water! It wafted gently, dipping and rising with smooth fluent movements. It was a ghostly body, pale and menacing, and it was right in the path of the boat. Robin and Aileen could hear the heavy, frightened breathing of the man at the wheel. He switched off the engine, watched for a few seconds more, then he stood on the side of the boat and jumped ashore. Aileen knew where they were. The boat had come to a halt at the beach below the Scroggy farm; the beach where she had first found the Brod of Bres.

The man passed the prow of the boat and Aileen grabbed Robin's jacket.

"Come on! He's going to see what it is. We can jump

now," she whispered. They landed on the shingle with a crunch. The boatman whirled around but he only saw fleeing black shadows. Ahead, the ghostly body swayed and beckoned with wraith-like fingers, daring the very jittery boatman to come forward.

Aileen brought Robin up the rock steps that she knew so well and then on to the path that led to home and safety.

"What was that?" gasped Robin when it was safe for them to slow down. "Was it the Morrigan or Mathgen or what?"

"No," replied Aileen and Robin could see that she was laughing. "It was Aggie Scroggy."

The apparition had been no mystery to Aileen at all. She had recognised the white woollen shawl that Aggie Scroggy sometimes pulled over her shoulders when she went to do some evening chore around the farm. Draped over a particularly protruding branch it had made a very convincing ghost.

Back home Aileen was late for dinner but Aggie Scroggy was even later.

"I forgot the time," said Aileen by way of explanation.

"I thought something was bothering the lambs," smiled Aggie when she arrived a few minutes later. She calmly took her place in the kitchen and began to serve the dinner. Not a hair on her head had stirred and she didn't even glance in Aileen's direction. Claire looked at her daughter and then at her mother-in-law and she guessed that the pair shared some secret that they were not going to tell. Then she sat down to eat.

An eyebrow was raised too when Robin came home late and obviously a bit shaken.

"Where were you till this time?" asked his worried mother.

"Out," replied Robin because he could think of nothing else to say.

"Well, you're here now," said Hugh Bradley. "Put out the dinner there Rosaleen. I'm starving."

Throughout the meal Robin could see that his grandfather had a juicy piece of news up his sleeve that he was just dying to blurt out. But he didn't. He savoured it and didn't talk until the moment was just right.

"There was a bit of a tragedy in the school today I hear," he said when the teapot was on the table and his mug was steaming. Robin couldn't think what he was talking about.

"I met Lambeg, Mr Quinn, in the village this evening and he was telling me all about it."

"Oh, yes," said Robin when he finally realised what his grandfather was talking about. "It was really bad. Poor Willie."

"Lambeg is near demented trying to find a substitute for Wee Willie," said Hugh.

"Is that right?" asked Robin as he slipped the chocolate biscuit out from the pile of custard creams.

"He was a bit surprised when I told him that the answer to all his problems was right under his nose."

The chocolate biscuit never reached Robin's mouth.

"What did you say to him, Granda?" he asked but he knew the answer already.

"I just told him," said Hugh Bradley proudly, "that he had in his school the Junior League Champion and top scorer of the whole north of England. And If he was looking for a striker he should look no further than

Robin Drake. He didn't believe me at first but I had a photo from a newspaper to show him. I keep it in my pocket."

"And did he say that he would give him a try?" asked Rosaleen pleased that her son's talents were at last going to be recognised.

"A try!" hooted Hugh Bradley. "He's away home the happiest man in Drumenny. I think he'll be looking for you tomorrow, Robin."

The two faces beamed their pleasure across the table and Robin hadn't the heart to tell them how he felt.

"That's great," he said and escaped to his room as soon as possible. Once there he kicked every piece of furniture and every box that filled the room. He didn't give a toss whether Drumenny School won the cup or not and he could just imagine the faces of the Battler Gang when Lambeg told them who their new team mate might be.

Robin wasn't to be disappointed. When Lambeg called Robin Drake to come out to the field to try out for the school team there was a stunned silence in the classroom. Aileen Kennedy was the most amazed of all.

"I have no kit, sir," said Robin feebly.

"Never mind that," bawled Lambeg. "We'll find something to fit you."

The changing-room was a hut that was possibly going to be a computer room some day but in the meantime it was stocked with surplus desks and tattered books that had outlived their usefulness. A pair of boots, at least two sizes too big, were found for Robin. He kept his head down while he laced them up but he could hear the mutterings from the other boys.

"Lambeg's lost his marbles," he heard.

"What could that scalped rabbit know about football?"

"We'll make poundies out of him," suggested Battler as he led the team out to the field.

Robin did not know what poundies were but he soon discovered that brute force was required in the making of them. If he made a half-hearted attempt to go for the ball at all there was an elbow in his face or a boot at his ankle. He didn't want to shine, the last thing he needed was to be picked for the team, but at the same time he didn't want to make a fool of his grandfather in front of Lambeg. And then he had his feet to contend with. He tried to tell them to mind their own business and not to be doing anything fancy but every now and again they were tempted and they danced off, delighted to feel the spring of the grass and the bounce of the ball.

At the end of the try-out Lambeg was perplexed. Hugh Bradley was not a man given to untruth or exaggeration so he had expected to see a blistering performance from young Robin Drake. Instead the boy had pussy-footed about avoiding trouble that nevertheless always seemed to find him. He was tempted to cross Robin off his list of possibles but then he thought again. In the middle of all the messing he had witnessed fleeting moments of pure genius, moments when the boy and the ball seemed to be one. Robin's feet had played with the ball manoeuvring it deftly away from plodding boots and trickling it down the field until the clever footwork was swamped in a pile of bodies from both sides. Time was running out and Lambeg made his decision.

"Drake, you will turn out for the team on the 18th."

There was an explosion of disgust from Battler Doherty and Ronan McCafferty.

"Do I take it that you boys are not entirely in agreement with my decision?" asked Lambeg mildly.

"Well, sir," said Battler, "he's yellow. He won't get stuck in."

"Maybe that is an advantage," smiled Lambeg.

"And . . . and . . . sir . . . well . . . like . . . he's not really from Drumenny at all, is he?" mumbled Ronan McCafferty.

"Explain yourself," demanded Lambeg.

"Sir . . . it's the way he . . . well, listen to him, sir! Just listen to the poncy way he talks! He's a Brit, sir!"

This conversation was taking place in the store room that the footballers used for changing and in the full hearing of Robin who was shaking off his football boots. Lambeg stood, rolling on his feet and hands in pockets. He didn't answer immediately. He rocked a bit more and then he spoke. His voice was so quiet that it shocked the boys into rigid attention.

"McCafferty," he said, "did you cheer for the Irish team when they did so well for us in the World Cup?"

"Yes sir."

"And did you listen to any of them being interviewed afterwards?"

"Yes sir."

"What did you think of their accents?"

McCafferty said nothing.

"Bit of a mixed bag, were they not?" said the headmaster mildly. "In fact I would say quite a few of them were decidedly 'poncy', to use your term. Am I not right, McCafferty?"

McCafferty hung his head.

"Drake, I will expect you in full strip tomorrow," roared Lambeg satisfied that he had convinced the grumblers.

So whether he liked it or not, and he didn't, Robin was on the Drumenny football team and playing in the cup final on the day after St Patrick's Day.

"You never told me," said Aileen in a huffy voice.

"What?"

"About the football."

"What about it?"

"That you could play and all."

"I played a bit."

Aileen sniffed. She felt that if she knew Robin Drake for a hundred years she still wouldn't know him at all. Then she forgot about the football. They had other things to talk about. They had to find the Brod of Bres before it was shipped out of the country.

"Everybody is after it now," said Aileen tugging at her hair. "The police are looking for it, and the Morrigan, and I suppose Mathgen is doing *something* about it too."

The children were sitting on the Brooding Rock. It was Aileen's special place on the beach below the Scroggy farm; the same beach that they had scrambled up the evening before. They had found Aggie's shawl where it had been tossed into a rock pool and had searched for signs of the boat but the Lough was silent and empty.

"Well, let's go over what we know," said Robin getting down to business. "We know that there are at least three people involved. There's Vale Prentess, the man in the boat and the mystery man . . . er . . . person."

"Yes, and we definitely know that they're going to use that boat. But when? And where will the boat be when they smuggle the Brod and the Stone on board?" asked Aileen. "Lough Foyle is fourteen miles long and there are loads of places to hide."

"They're going to do it right in the middle of Derry," decided Robin. "Remember what was said about traffic – it has to be in the town."

"But there's always loads of traffic in Derry," sighed Aileen, "and what difference does traffic make to a boat anyway?"

"God knows," said Robin. "We haven't got very far have we? But we'd need to come up with something soon. Vale Prentess said there wasn't much time left."

"I think you're right about Vale selling the Brod," said Aileen. "Did you see her face when she saw the crow? The Morrigan is after her and the Brod but we've got to get there first."

∿ The Pageant ∿

One day it was winter with its cheek-chafing frosts and bone-chilling gales, the next a gentle breeze blew, the sun shone and spring had arrived. Winter *could* make an entrance again for it is loath to release its hold on the rocky, sea-blasted northern tip of Ireland, but in the meantime brave buds tipped the trees, birds sang in courtship and lambs frolicked in the fields.

Robin had not seen Cloughderg in such calm and soothing weather and the beauty and magnificence of the scenery captivated him. The waves rolled in from the Atlantic in regular well-tamed rows and washed over the black rocks leaving neat frills of white froth. High-fronted trawlers, taking advantage of the good weather, loaded their nets and chugged out to the mouth of the Lough and then on to deeper waters. Even Cloughderg Mountain looked less grim and unfriendly as the new springing of grass and early shootings of wild plants softened the rock faces.

Contentment should have been soothing Robin's worried brow but it was not. Much as he enjoyed finding new places to explore and challenging rocks to climb he could not get the dread of the cup final match out of his mind. There had been two more practices with the team and he had the bruises to prove it.

Lambeg was looking at him as if he realised he had made a terrible mistake but was not going to admit it.

He didn't care about the hammering he was bound to get during the match nor about Lambeg's low opinion; what did matter to him was the disappointment of his mother and grandfather. Hugh Bradley had been bragging to every customer who had brought a machine to his shed, or who had sent for him to come and fix one, that his grandson was going to give a display of football never before seen in Drumenny.

His own football gear wasn't the school colour so he had been given Wee Willie Clements's strip and his mother had lovingly washed and ironed every item and now it was sitting folded in tissue paper in a drawer awaiting the great day. She had rubbed and buffed his footies until they were fit for Wembley and they were sitting proudly on the dressing table. Of course they would both be there. How could they miss seeing Robin cheered on by his school friends?

Aileen knew how much Robin dreaded the match and she tried to keep his mind off it. Every chance she got she brought up the subject of the Brod of Bres. Two days had passed and they were no nearer to discovering the time and place when the great carved stone and the little two-faced statue would be smuggled out of the country. The Brod could have gone already or the Morrigan could have it in her grasping talons. It might even be safe with Mathgen. These were all possibilities but Aileen believed that the Brod of Bres was still somewhere in Derry. She felt that if anything tremendous had happened to it she would know.

"Should we tell the police what we know?" asked Robin as they sat on a rock watching the sea gulls gather in the wake of a trawler.

"But we don't know anything really," answered Aileen. "How could we explain to them about Vale Prentess? And we have no proof that she has the Stone or the Brod."

Round and round in circles they went but they only ended up more and more confused.

Things were fairly hectic in school too. Mrs McCloskey had received a final programme of events for the Spirit of the Foyle Festival and she was twittering with nerves.

"It will be a very full day," she told the class. "In the afternoon there will be the street events and the history of the river will be told in living pageant. The myths will come first and we will be on second. It is all very well organised and if everybody behaves it should go well. In the evening there will be the parade of boats on the river. As well as our canoe there will be currachs and longships, brigantines and barques. There will also be a US naval gunboat, one similar to those that were in Derry during the war."

The teacher went on to explain that when all the ships had gathered the beautiful statue, The Spirit of the Foyle, would be lowered by crane on to the little island that had been specially built for her in the middle of the river. Then the evening would be rounded off with a magnificent fireworks display.

"A Day in the Life of a Stone Age Village" had been practised until the children could do it in their sleep. They'd had rehearsals with a professional actor who was the narrator for the Historical Pageant. He would

99

pretend that he was a visitor from the present time and would ask the children to explain what they were doing. Lisa McCarron and Nuala Deery still grumbled about their costumes but they had speaking parts so they were quite contented. Battler Doherty and all the bigger boys got to stand around looking wild and fierce with their long shafted spears and their belts weighed down with axes, so they were fairly happy too. The smallest in the class, including Robin and Aileen, would play children's games with pebbles or string bone beads onto strips of leather. The two children had nothing to say and they were relieved.

St Patrick's Day arrived and, with shamrocks sprouting from lapels, hat bands or best frocks, the people headed to churches all over the country, smiled greetings to their neighbours and prepared to enjoy the National Holiday. Some would go to a race meeting, some to a football match, some to the pub and some would enjoy lying around the house taking their leisure. There were parades in most towns but by far the greatest show in the north-west, and maybe even in all of Ireland, would be the Spirit of the Foyle Festival in Derry city.

After hearty dinners, crowds began to converge on the city from all the outlying villages. The Scroggys set off early so as to beat the traffic. They had to go quite slowly because Hugh Bradley was following them and he had the dug-out canoe sticking out of the back of his van.

Aileen and Robin, already dressed for the pageant, were jammed in the front seat beside Hugh, and Rosaleen was in the Scroggy car. The children quite liked their costumes and they weren't itchy at all.

Although they looked rough, Aileen's mother had lined the woollen tunics so that they were smooth to the touch. The skin boots had been massaged with many coats of baby oil and they were soft and comfortable on the feet. The best part of dressing up was the tangling of the hair and the dirtying of faces. Usually they had to dress in their best going out for the day and then keep themselves clean. Despite all their worries the children were excited.

As the city centre was closed to traffic people had to park in the many makeshift car parks provided for the visitors. It was odd to see the roads teeming with people and not a car or lorry in sight. Even the busy dual carriageway behind the Guildhall was taken over by jubilant revellers.

There was a great air of celebration about the city. Most of the shops, except for the cafés and pubs, were closed and the thoroughfares were decorated in gay banners and criss-crossed with necklaces of brightly coloured bunting. The streets were packed and most people were in costume. There were Vikings sucking ice pops and cowled monks eating bags of chips; Elizabethan English gentlemen in their puffy pantaloons and wrinkled tights chatted to bare-legged Celts with flowing false moustaches. There were soldiers and sailors from every century mixing with shawled emigrants in their tattered clothes carrying bundles of meagre belongings.

The street carnival was supposed to start at half two, but it was three and after it before Aileen and Robert heard the strains of the first band coming down the steep slope of Shipquay Street, through a gate in the ancient walls and into Guildhall Square. Giants, made from papier mâché and ten feet tall, did battle with a great clashing of wooden staffs or growled at toddlers who roared with delight. Clowns with white painted faces and baggy trousers squirted water at the crowd and clowns on stilts juggled coloured balls. There was a fire eater and a sword swallower and troupes of dancers in outlandish costumes. There were flute bands and pipe bands, jazz bands and brass bands and everyone was having a whale of a time.

Then through the gate came a monstrous head. A black forked tongue flicked from the evil mouth, skimming the crowd. All the children screamed. Into the square came the monster and now the crowd could see that it was supposed to be a snake. A hundred pairs of feet twisted and turned under the grotesque snakeskin and the reptile began to weave its way around the square threatening all in its path with its lashing tongue. It was indeed a prodigious beast. It almost filled the square and the tail was still coming in through the gate.

A roar of rage was heard and all looked up. A huge St Patrick stood high up on the city walls and the snake cowered in fright. The Saint was lowered to the ground on pulleys and a great battle began. The snake hissed and the crowd booed. St Patrick waved his crosier and the crowd cheered. After many fierce skirmishes the snake was finally vanquished. It lay in a long exhausted stream of tangled legs and mangled papier mâché. Children climbed on to the wreckage and tore off strips of skin as souvenirs. St Patrick did a lap of honour around the square and he was loudly congratulated for his performance.

It was now time for a short break as saint and snake

went to drown their shamrocks. A stage had been set up outside the Guildhall and it was there that the school children would perform. Someone was testing the loudspeaker system. The children who were acting out the first scene were already gathering on the stage and from the bottom of the steps Lambeg could be heard summoning the Drumenny pupils to his side. He did not need to avail himself of the loudspeaker.

An expectant buzz filled the square as the people waited for the next part of the Festival – the Living History Pageant. The mayor of the city welcomed everybody to the Spirit of the Foyle Festival and thanked a long list of people for the hard work that had ensured success. Then she announced the second part of the Festival which was the contribution from all the schools of the city and many beyond its boundaries. She thanked all the teachers and parents involved, promised the crowd that they were in for a treat and the Living Story of the Foyle began.

The narrator introduced the first scene and explained that the Foyle was rich in legends and myths and that the first scene would tell the story of the Children of Lir.

The story was told in mime and was accompanied by haunting music played on flute, pipes and bodhrán. The three beautiful children, beloved of their father, Lir, were changed into swans by their jealous stepmother and condemned to a life afloat until they heard the tinkle of a Christian bell. For nine hundred years they waited and, according to legend, three hundred of those years were spent on Lough Foyle.

The children were given a great clap and were roundly congratulated by proud parents and then it was the turn of Drumenny School. Props were carried on to the stage and the pupils arranged themselves in their groups. Robin and Aileen settled themselves comfortably at the back of the stage and the story began.

The Narrator told the crowd how the first farmers had come to the Foyle and remains of their presence had been found in sites all over the north of the country. He explained how important the Foyle would have been to a Stone Age community both as a source of food and for transport. Canoes similar to the one they would see later that evening had been found in the upper reaches of the river.

He moved among the busy children as a modern reporter transported to another age. He chatted easily to them and they were so well rehearsed that the carefully scripted interviews appeared completely impromptu. Everything was going very well with Lisa and Nuala speaking in their elocution voices and Battler sharpening his spear and scanning the crowd with a fierce eye looking for likely prey.

Aileen's mind drifted away. She played with her little pebbles and as she looked at them they shimmered and changed into a clear image of the little Brod of Bres. She had an overpowering sense of the presence of the Brod somewhere nearby. The feeling was so strong that she dropped the pebbles and they went scattering over the stage almost causing the narrator to lose his footing.

"What's up?" asked Robin for Aileen had taken a long breath and had gone very pale. She was staring out into the crowd.

"She's there," whispered Aileen. Robin followed the

direction of her gaze and his eyes came to rest on the sharp features of Vale Prentess.

"She has the Brod," said Aileen. "I just know she has."

The scene came to an end and children came down the steps to be ushered quickly away so that the next group could perform.

Although Lambeg and Mrs McCloskey were beside themselves with praise and pride the teacher smiled stiffly at Aileen and said, "Pity about those pebbles, Aileen. But, accidents will happen."

"It's today!" said Aileen in a ferment of excitement. "They are going to move the Stone and the Brod today."

"But that doesn't make sense," replied a puzzled Robin. "She definitely said there would be loads of traffic about and there's none at all in the town today – plenty of people, but no traffic."

"I don't care," said Aileen. "The Brod will be taken out of the country today. I just know it. And I'll tell you who else knows it – Mathgen!"

"Mathgen! But how can you tell that?"

"There was another face in the crowd, right behind Vale Prentess. One minute it was there and the next it wasn't but I saw it and it was Mathgen!"

"Mathgen? Standing in the middle of the crowd?" asked an incredulous Robin. "But he hates people!"

"Well, he was there surrounded by thousands of them and he didn't look a bit out of place."

Robin scanned the crowd hoping to see the flowing white hair and beard of the druid. There were plenty of faces with beards and moustaches and plenty of men dressed in skirts and cloaks but none of them was

Mathgen. Vale Prentess was still there. She appeared to be very absorbed in the stage performances and was standing near the front of the crowd.

"We'll watch her," suggested Robin. "If she is up to anything then we'll know about it."

They sidled into the crowd and positioned themselves near enough to Vale Prentess to keep her in their sights. Now that she was closer to the girl, Aileen had an almost overwhelming feeling of the nearness of the Brod. She was determined that no matter what happened that day, the Brod would not leave the country – nor would it fall into the hands of the Morrigan.

∞ The Grand Finale ∞

It took over an hour for the school children to tell the whole history of Life on the Foyle. They told of people who had sailed up the river to raid or to settle and people who had sailed down the river to escape hunger or to chase a dream. Vale Prentess watched every scene and the two children watched Vale Prentess. It was already beginning to get dark when the performance drew to a close. The narrator announced a break of one hour and then the Grand Finale of the Festival would take place behind the Guildhall on the river itself.

There was a great rush to find seats in the cafés and Robin and Aileen found themselves pushed this way and that in the milling throng. And of course they lost sight of Vale Prentess.

"She's got away from us," said Robin in dismay. "We'll never find her now."

"I think we will," said Aileen. "I have a feeling about it. But I'm starving with hunger now. Come on!"

A few minutes later the children sat in the back of Hugh Bradley's van with the door open and their legs dangling over the side.

"Eat up quickly," said Aileen as she wolfed down an egg and onion roll. "I think we should get back to the Guildhall as soon as possible."

"I'm going as fast as I can," replied Robin through a mouth full of coleslaw.

People were crowded on to all the wrought iron seats in the Square, on the steps of all the buildings and on the fountain in Waterloo Place that led off the Square. Fairy lights were strung between the ornamental trees and knots of people had gathered round groups of street musicians.

There was music to please every taste. Some danced to a lively reel played on fiddle and tin whistle while others gyrated to the rhythm of a small rock band. A classical guitarist had drawn a rapt audience and some children were captivated by the mad antics of a one-man band. The stage had been taken over and undiscovered pop stars were performing for an amused and very disrespectful audience.

Behind the Guildhall the final preparations were being made for the Parade of Boats and the Grand Finale. Stands of tiered seating had been set up in the dual carriageway and in any open spaces beside the river. Many people had already taken their seats and others were lining the railed section along the river and filling every available place along the quays. The river was in total darkness.

The children found a gap in the crowd at the quayside and they hooked their arms over the rail and stared out into the blackness. Suddenly a barrage of laser beams streaked through the night and lit up the river. It was alive with boats! Each was illuminated for a fleeting second in the spotlights. The images passed before the children's eyes like stills from a Hollywood film. They saw their own dug-out canoe manned by hairy adventurers from Drumenny, a Viking longship and a sturdy Celtic sailing boat, both bristling with warriors, and a currach crewed by Colm Cille and his cowled monks. Barques, brigs and sloops, created by engineering and artistic genius, rocked beside the gunmetal grey of a US Navy gunboat.

St Patrick, recovered from his joust, was balanced on a raft anchored to two small tugs and waiting to play his part in the Finale. From a tall crane a large shrouded figure dangled and swayed. It was the Spirit of the Foyle waiting to be lowered on to her little man-made island. Two barges, stuffed with fireworks, were floating quietly alongside her final resting place.

The lights continued to play over the river and the small craft had their moment of glory. Fancy power boats jostled with modest punts and half-deckers, and jet skiers zipped and darted among them like night flying wasps. Harbour police struggled to keep control of the busyness of the river and olive green army dories swayed silently in the shadows. Then the lights went out and blackness returned. The technicians had had their practice and now the real performance would begin.

"Did you see it?" asked Robin

Aileen nodded. The last spotlight had signed off with a final flourish over the crowd at the edge of the quay. It lit up the dark waters that flowed at their feet. Not ten yards away from where Robin and Aileen were standing a boat was tied up to the very last rail. It was not part of the riotous river celebrations; it was the boat they had boarded at Lloyd's Bank.

Now that the lights had gone out they could no longer see the boat but they knew exactly where it was.

"That's it!" said Robin. "It's the river that's full of

traffic, not the roads! They will sneak on board with the Stone and the Brod and with all the noise and fuss nobody will pay any attention to one boat slipping off into the darkness."

They moved along the rail and stood looking at the boat. The bow was rising and dipping about a foot below the quay wall.

"I don't think there is anybody on it," said Aileen.

"I want to take a look," said Robin and he stepped down on to the narrow ledge that skirted the cabin windows. The boat rocked a little and he steadied himself against the wall. Then he guided Aileen safely aboard.

The space below decks was empty. They tried to explore the cabin but in the darkness it was impossible to see very much. There was a table and a sink and a cooker and built-in seating. Beyond the galley another door led to a small toilet and beyond that was a tiny triangular bunk room, just big enough to crawl into. They squeezed into it and from the window they looked out on to the river. The parade of boats had begun and the laser beams danced over the waters. They had a perfect view of the marvellous spectacle.

"Colm Cille is taking off now, with his monks to Iona," said Aileen. "The Vikings will be next."

They watched enthralled as each boat was introduced to the spectators. Brawny Vikings brandished heavy broadswords and weeping emigrants fluttered scraps of rags in sad farewells.

Suddenly the boat rocked violently under the weight of a heavy boot.

"Ease it down over the side and I'll keep it steady," came a voice they recognised. It was the man who had been on the boat at Lloyd's Bank.

"Careful now. If it is broken we will lose a lot of money."

This was a different voice and it bothered Aileen. She had heard it before but she couldn't remember where or when.

"I don't know why we couldn't have waited another few days," grumbled the same voice. "There must be more stones like this in that tunnel. I could have organised a team to get them out."

Now Aileen knew who it was! It was Professor Clayton with his very distinctive voice.

"And that would risk losing what we've got," retorted Vale Prentess angrily. "Between the Stone and the little statue we should make a fair packet. That's if we can get away with it. Is it safe to move yet?"

"I think the time is just about right," replied the boatman. The engine was switched on and in the little triangular bunk-room two frightened children shivered as the boat slipped away from the quayside and out into the dark waters of the river. From their little window they watched as the bright lights and flotilla of boats, surrounded by small craft, disappeared from sight. The boat was moving in total darkness now and the engine was throbbing quietly.

It was so dark in their hidey-hole that they could only see teeth and whites of eyes.

"We should have stayed on the quay and watched for them coming," whispered Robin. "Then we could have told the police and got them stopped."

"Great idea," answered Aileen, "but just a bit too late."

The sound of their voices was drowned by the hum

of the engine but this worked both ways and they could no longer hear the conversation of the trio on deck.

On the boat chugged and the children looked longingly at the twinkling lights of the houses that lined the bank of the river. They passed under the Foyle Bridge and the lights began to thin out. The river broadened into the Lough and now they could only see black water and an odd pinpoint of light very far away on the dim horizon.

"Where will we end up?" asked Robin. "And what will they do with us when they find us?"

"I don't know," replied Aileen, "but at least we know where the Brod is. And I will do everything I can to keep it away from the Morrigan."

The words had hardly left her mouth when there was a great churning in the river and the water began to bubble and froth like a pot on the boil. The boat was whipped out of the water and then tossed carelessly back again. Framed in the window of the tiny bunk-room was an eye – huge and yellow and terrible.

The children were thrown into the galley and on out through the open cabin doors. Three bodies, in a state of profound shock, were sprawled on the floor of the boat. Their stunned eyes looked at the children as they landed in a heap beside them and then all five looked at the boiling waters. A huge head nudged at the boat until it shuddered violently. It was a monstrous head with one eye on each side of a flat forehead and a long, narrow crocodile mouth lined with regimented rows of teeth. Nostrils, like black holes, flared at the snubbed end of the vicious mouth.

"It's her!" came the terrified shriek of Vale Prentess. "The Shape-shifter!"

The scaly body of the monster breached the waters and a stiff frill of bony spikes bristled a warning from the broad, powerful back. Three tails, each ribbed with slicing barbs, flicked into sight then vanished again in a thunderous splash.

The boatman was the first to recover. He cursed loudly, pushed the engine to full throttle and swung round in a crazy arc. The boat leaned over until it was almost on its side and then it skited away – almost swallowed up in a curving arch of silvered water. The passengers were thrown from one side of the boat to the other but when it finally steadied they looked over the side. They could no longer see the yellow eyes and muscular body.

"Cut the engine!" ordered Professor Clayton. He grabbed Aileen by the back of her tunic, almost strangling her, and for a moment he didn't recognise her in her Stone Age get-up. Then his breath escaped in a hiss through his clenched teeth.

"It's that brat who was in the tunnel. The one with the bad memory. What are these two doing on the boat?"

"We have more to worry us than those two pests," snapped Vale. "We have to get out of here fast – or all hell will break loose!"

The water was calm and nothing now disturbed its oily black surface. The engine was switched on again and the throttle eased gently forward. The boat turned and began to inch slowly out towards the mouth of the Lough. The water still glistened smooth and unbroken. Vale Prentess sat hunched at the side of the boat peering into the darkness. Her body was straining with tension. No one moved or spoke, fearing that even the sound of a breath would rouse whatever lurked in the shadowy depths.

The boat slid past the scene of the attack and there was great relief on board.

"Did we see anything at all?" asked Professor Clayton. "Or did we all have a wild hallucination?"

In answer to his question the great three-pronged tail came flashing over the boat drenching the cowering bodies with slimy water. Then the monstrous head reappeared. This time it was level with the boat and from the nostrils steamed putrid vapour. The beast raised its head and stayed poised over the trembling beings as if enjoying their terror. Then slowly the head descended and the slitted mouth opened. Teeth flashed as the grinning mouth prepared to crush the boat and its occupants.

Again the boatman swung the boat round and they could hear the gnashing of the teeth as the mouth closed on emptiness. They roared off at full power back towards the city lights. Behind the beleaguered boat the tip of a dark head could be seen as it charged in pursuit; two waves of white froth streamed from the nostrils and two yellow eyes glowed in the darkness.

Back under the Foyle Bridge they went and now ahead they could see the hordes of boats and the shrouded figure of the Spirit of the Foyle as it floated in a blaze of light above the river.

"That thing could have caught us by now!" shouted the boatman. "It's playing with us! What does it want anyway?"

"I know what she wants. And she can have it!"

Only Aileen heard Vale Prentess speak as the girl began to fumble blindly in her pocket.

The boat was now hurtling at full speed through the water weaving a crazy passage between the small boats and scattering them in all directions. Angry fists were waved and threatening curses were lost in the hullabaloo. They were now in the middle of the festival boats and approaching the dangling statue. The Harbour Police boat was steaming towards the tearaway vessel and an army dory was also skimming over the water in pursuit.

Vale Prentess had struggled to her feet. She raised her arm.

"Take it!" she shouted. "Take it and leave me in peace!"

Aileen lunged forward to stop her but she was too late. A small object went flying out over the water. It curved away in a high arc and just as it dipped towards the water a dark shape flew up out of the water and into the night. A small object was imprisoned in its beak. Aileen had failed. The Morrigan had the Brod of Bres!

A lone trumpet played a fanfare and wild cheering broke out from the crowds lining both sides of the Foyle. Laser beams now criss-crossed to illuminate the ceremony of the unveiling of the Spirit of the Foyle. The shroud was whipped away to reveal a young girl in swirling dress and flowing tresses. A dove, carrying a sprig of oak leaf, nestled on her shoulder. She looked delicate and beautiful but she weighed a ton. Slowly the crane began to lower her into her final resting place in midstream where she would stand, with bronze arms outstretched, to welcome all who sailed in peace on her river.

The careering half-decker was now surrounded by

army dorys and Harbour Police boats and could go no further. With a sigh of defeat the boatman cut the engine. Robin and Aileen stared in anguish out over the busy water. They had messed everything up. Now that the Morrigan had the Brod she could go in search of the Evil Eye of Balor and, with the terrible power that she would then gain, unleash dreadful horrors on all the worlds!

Suddenly a small but sturdy ship slid across their bow. It was a sailing ship of ancient design and on its prow stood a majestic figure with a mane of white hair and a flowing beard.

"It's Mathgen!" shouted Robin.

"But what can he do?" gasped an anguished Aileen. "The Brod has gone."

Mathgen raised his rod and the clear crystal stone vibrated with pure light. A thin beam of unnatural brightness sliced into the night sky. It found and followed a black dot. High up above the heads of the revellers there was a tiny blast of pure white light and something began to fall down and down into the blare of the laser beams. Only three pairs of eyes saw the small object fall from the sky into the dark hole. One split second later the Spirit of the Foyle was placed on her little island home. Her dainty bare feet stood firm and sure on her pedestal, covering forever the Brod of Bres!

There was a moment of awed silence and then a series of sharp blasts ripped from the floating barges. Fireworks streaked off in every direction and exploded high above the river in showers of coloured stars. A rope was tied to the half-decker and it was towed towards the quay by an army dory. Unnoticed by the excited crowds, the bedraggled passengers climbed on to the quay wall and, while the sky danced in shattered rainbows, three adults and an ancient stone slab were loaded into a police van.

๑ The Calming of the Waters ๑

What a night Aileen and Robin had after that! There were explanations to be invented and a thousand questions to be avoided.

"We were just playing on the boat when it took off," said Robin, wide-eyed with innocence.

Aileen nodded in agreement and then she added breathlessly, "And then the boat just seemed to go out of control and we were thrown all over the place and we just didn't know what was happening!"

The authorities accepted their story, warned them of the dangers of playing near boats and then carted off the thieves and their booty. The families were scolding the children one minute and then, relieved that they were safe on dry land, wrapping them in bear hugs the next. A small section of the crowd gathered round thinking that the activity was part of the Grand Finale but most of the people were watching the fireworks and didn't witness any of the drama at the quayside. Later, they would open the *Derry Journal* and read all about the recovery of the stolen Grianan Stone and then they would tell everybody that they were there and saw it all happening.

Just before the little group from Cloughderg left the quayside to pile into their vehicles and head for home,

Aggie Scroggy gently placed her frail hand on Aileen's arm. Aileen looked up into the young-old face and she saw that Aggie Scroggy knew everything that had happened that night.

"Look over there," whispered the old woman. The fireworks display was over and the crowd was thinning out. A lonely figure, an ancient Celt, sat humped and dejected on one of the fancy seats beside the fountain. It was Mathgen!

Aileen slipped away from Aggie and went to join the old Druid. She sat beside him quietly for a few seconds but he didn't seem to notice her. Then she tugged at his sleeve gently.

"Cheer up," she said. "It's not the end of the world."

"Ah, Aileen the Fair," said a woebegone Mathgen as he shook his head sadly. "It may not be the end of *your* world," he sighed, "but it just could be the end of mine. The Brod of Bres was given into the care of the Children of Light by our mother Danu and I, Mathgen, Chief Druid to all the Kings, I have lost it. It is in a prison made by mortals. It has gone beyond the power of my High Magic."

"The Brod isn't lost," said Aileen as she searched for words to comfort Mathgen. "It's just not available at the moment – sort of out of circulation. And if you can't get at it then neither can the Morrigan. In fact I can't think of a safer place for the Brod to be than under the heel of the Spirit of the Foyle!"

Mathgen's head shot up and he stared at the girl sitting by his side patting his hand.

"That is true," he said. "The Low Magic of the Morrigan will not free the Brod. It is imprisoned under

119

the feet of a lady almost as fair as the Danu herself."

For a moment his brow cleared then it darkened again.

"But it is a prison that is in the keeping of mortals and wherever there are mortals . . . "

"I know, I know! There is always trouble," interrupted Aileen. "But, listen to me. The Brod was under the ocean with Manaanan Mac Lir and it got lost. Isn't that right?"

Mathgen nodded dumbly.

"And it was under the Grianan of Aileach with the sleeping warriors and it got lost. Isn't that right?"

Again Mathgen nodded.

"As long as you lot keep losing it then there is always the danger that the Morrigan will find it and use it to open the Evil Eye of Balor and then the Fomar will be your masters. Isn't that right?"

This time the nod was barely noticeable.

"Well then," said Aileen with the air of one who has just proved an important point, "it just could be that the Brod is safer now than it's ever been since the end of the wars between the Fomar and the Danu. Maybe it is the turn of the mortals to look after it?"

The old Druid stood up and looked towards the lovely statue on her lonely island in the middle of the river. Her face and outstretched arms were illuminated by a circle of little spotlights that nestled at her feet and she seemed to float above the water.

"I hope you are right," he said doubtfully but he sounded a bit more cheerful.

"Of course I'm right," said Aileen. "I'm glad that the Brod fell where it did. It couldn't be in a better place. It will be safe in its little hidey-hole for . . . for . . . well, forever!"

"Forever!" said Mathgen smiling for the first time. "And tell me, Aileen the Fair, what does forever mean?"

"Well . . . it means just going on and on and . . . and . . . never stopping," stuttered Aileen but she stopped when she saw that Mathgen's blue eyes were laughing at her. She blushed at her foolishness in trying to explain "forever" to someone who lived in a world beyond time.

Mathgen put his arm round her shoulder and gave her a gentle squeeze.

"We will see," he said. "We will see how long the Brod of Bres lies in safety with mortals. But in the meantime we have averted danger and thwarted the Morrigan and her evil designs once again. I must be grateful for that and for your help in finding the Brod. Now I must go back to my world. Perhaps the danger is finally over. Perhaps the Morrigan will abandon her evil quest now and all our worlds can finally rest in peace."

The voice was soothing and kind but the expression on Mathgen's face told Aileen that he was really trying to convince himself.

"It could be so," he said gently. "We may have heard the last of the Morrigan and the little Brod of Bres may lie safely beneath the pretty feet of the Spirit of the Foyle – forever."

"Aileen!" shouted Robin Drake as he sprinted across the cobbles, "Aileen, we are going now . . . "

He stopped dead in his tracks when he saw Mathgen.

"It is Robin of the Questions himself," beamed the Druid. "Just in time to say farewell."

For a brief moment Mathgen rested a hand on each head before he turned and walked towards the river. Then he was swallowed up in the darkness.

❦ The Great Final ❦

Aileen Kennedy was feeling contented. Ever since the Brod of Bres had come into her life she had felt that she was honour-bound to protect it from the evil schemes of the Morrigan. Now, despite Mathgen's doubts, it was as if a great weight had been lifted from her shoulders. She was sure that the Brod was safe at last under the delicately carved feet of the Spirit of the Foyle.

Robin Drake, however, was far from happy. It was Saturday the 18th of March, the day after the Foyle Festival, and the Interschools cup final match would take place in Drumenny village that afternoon. Robin was sick with dread and burdened with a whole range of unpleasant emotions; some he recognised and others he couldn't put a name on. He was angry and afraid, bitter and resentful.

He blamed everybody for his predicament – his mother and father, Lambeg and his grandfather, but most of all he blamed Drumenny School. He hated the school and everyone in it except Aileen Kennedy. He did not want to play for Drumenny School. Why should he? All the pupils despised him. They had either joined in or watched silently each time Battler Doherty and his mates had had a go at him and they would gather in the football field to cheer as they made mincemeat out of him.

The pleased look on his mother's face as she packed his football kit and wished him luck had made Robin feel even more miserable. He knew what she was thinking. She was thinking, "everything is going to be all right now. He has settled in well. Isn't he on the school football team and playing in the final? His school friends must really like him and after today, when he has shown them what he can do with a ball, he will be even more popular." Robin couldn't find the words to tell his mother that she was fooling herself. But she would find out soon enough. She would be there to witness his humiliation.

It was a bright crisp afternoon and the ground was firm under foot – a perfect day for a football match. The field was at the end of the long village street. A stream of blue and gold was flowing towards the gate as supporters gathered carrying flags and banners and decked in hats, scarves and jumpers in the school colours. Two coaches were pulled up on the grass verge beside the field and a knot of red and black at the touch line indicated the opposition and their supporters.

Robin didn't even know the name of the school they were playing against and he couldn't care less. It was Termon something or other; one of those impossible tongue twisters of a name that seemed to be given to every other field in this country. Lambeg was prancing up and down the pitch in a lather of excitement and anxiety. A blue sweatshirt, with 'Drumenny School' emblazoned on it in gold lettering, strained to cover his solid stomach, and a blue and gold peaked cap was perched at a drunken angle on his massive head. Around his neck were strung a whistle, a stopwatch and a pencil and notebook. Perspiration dripped from his creased brow and his vocal chords were at full stretch.

Under Mrs McCloskey's direction, the school band was trying to entertain the crowd. The band consisted of four accordions, a French horn and two very squeaky trumpets, so only those in the immediate vicinity were aware that there was music being made at all.

The Drumenny team was warming up on the pitch, passing the ball with neat flicks of the foot or showy tosses of the head. The ball did not come in the direction of Robin Drake. He stood small and shivering outside the warmth of the cheery banter and backchat that binds a team together. Robin could see the faces in the crowd that he didn't want to see and then the whistle blew. He decided that he wouldn't look at those faces throughout the match.

For the first fifteen minutes there wasn't much action on the pitch at all. The teams were fairly evenly matched with big blocky defenders and small nippy forwards. Robin was playing on the outside wing and that is exactly where he was left – out on a limb and starved of the ball. There was a scuffle at the Drumenny goal mouth and a lucky ball bounced off a blue elbow and dribbled past a dismayed goalkeeper. Drumenny had scored a soft goal! The crowd went wild. Ten minutes later they scored again and as the half time whistle blew a very jaunty team waved to their cheering supporters and went to get their sliced oranges.

Lambeg was beside himself. "Ye have them, boys!" he roared slapping backs. "Just keep the pressure on and the cup is ours!"

Robin didn't take any orange; he hadn't done anything to raise a thirst. He could feel his mother's puzzled eyes boring into his back but he didn't turn round.

"It was hardly worth your while coming was it, Chookie Birdie?" yelled Battler Doherty loud enough for a fair section of the crowd to hear.

"Ach now, be fair," said Ronan McCafferty. "I saw the sleeve of his jersey once, sticking out behind that big gorilla of a defender. He didn't just mark our wee Brit, he blotted him out!"

"He's dead and doesn't know to lie down," came another voice.

"Naw, he's just yella," said another.

"Maybe he thinks we're playing hopscotch."

"He's afraid to get his nice gear dirty."

"Wait till you see," decided Battler. "He's saving the fancy stuff for the second half. He'll make it three, no bother."

"Naw," replied Ronan McCafferty wiping juice from his chin. "He couldn't score on a jotter."

The litany of insults went on but Robin pretended not to hear and looked away in the direction of the other team. Their coach had them in a huddle with arms linked and heads together, furiously planning their strategy for the second half.

"We'll keep their forwards pinned down this half," roared Lambeg announcing his intentions to the whole field. "Don't give them an inch and you should be making the most of every opportunity . . . "

Nobody was listening to Lambeg. The team's attention was concentrated on Battler Doherty and his whispered suggestions.

"I could beat this lot myself with one leg in plaster and the other asleep," he said. "They're dead meat. We'd need to liven things up or we'll all go into a coma. The fans could do with a bit of fun too or they'll start going home for their tea. We could have great crack with your man there . . . "

Robin didn't hear the plans but the sniggers and burst of loud laughter told him that he would not escape attention in the second half.

And he was right. As soon as the whistle blew the trouble began. This time the ball was passed to him frequently – usually when he was surrounded and immediately buried by a wall of red and black shirts. He got passes too when Battler Doherty was at hand to land a hefty kick on his shin before clearing the ball. They all came at him; some were even willing to be penalised for being off-side. The referee was bewildered. He raised the whistle once after a particularly vicious tackle from Ronan McCafferty but he didn't blow it. How could he penalise somebody for committing a foul against a member of his own team?

Battler and his gang were really enjoying themselves now and every time they sent Robin Drake flying or stuck an elbow in his face they waved and smirked at their schoolmates for approval. The supporters, however, were growing silent and there were few rewarding cheers. They shuffled their feet and dug their hands in their pockets and they began to lose their enthusiasm for the match.

Meantime, the opponents in red and black realised

that this hacking job on the wee fellow on the outside wing could be their golden opportunity and they began to take advantage of the situation. Their forwards were hardly being marked at all and next time they gained possession they were up the field in a flash and had scored a beautiful goal before the Drumenny team knew what was happening.

Still this did not frighten the gallant ten in blue and gold. They had their prey cornered and they wanted to play some more with him. The spectators by now had grown very restless. The adults were puzzled and disappointed but the children knew exactly what was happening. Aileen Kennedy was biting her finger nails. Every thump that Robin got made her flinch with anguish. Then she could stand it no more. The next time Robin was tackled she cupped her hands around her mouth and booed long and loud.

Battler heard her and turned with a sneer. He made a very rude sign in her direction. Aileen continued to boo and to her surprise she heard one or two voices joining in. The disapproval grew and soon it swelled to a mighty roar as hands were cupped around the booing mouths of all the school children. The Drumenny team was affronted by this display of disloyalty and as they stood and scratched their heads the ball once again slid into the net of the enemy and the score was even.

Robin Drake too heard the booing and at first he couldn't believe his ears. The pupils of Drumenny School were booing Battler Doherty and his henchmen! Then he heard a lone voice that he recognised take up another chant.

"Come on Robin!" shouted Aileen and a ragged half dozen voices joined in. Just at that moment his quick eye saw a loose ball and an outside chance. He hesitated for a fraction of a second and then he took off. He dribbled and he dodged, weaving circles round players twice his size. He sent the ball away at an angle from the interfering boots of towering defenders and miraculously he was there to take it up again on a dancing toe. He was down the field like quicksilver leaving a trail of beaten warriors in his wake and with deadly accuracy his right foot belted the ball past the left ear of the goal keeper and into the net to put Drumenny a goal ahead.

The crowd went mad! They were throwing caps in the air and hoisting banners in a frenzy of excitement. But the final whistle had not blown yet! The blood was up in Robin Drake now, fuelled by the pure joy of really playing football again. He behaved outrageously, showing off like a matador in a bullring and running rings round every player on the field.

A new chant had started and Robin smiled when he heard it.

"CHOOKEE BIRDEE! CHOOKEE BIRDEE!" came the war cry and even Lambeg took it up. To cut a long story short, Robin scored a hat trick before the match was over and so was an instant hero. His nickname was now a badge of honour and was used fondly and with pride by the victorious Drumenny supporters.

At the presentation ceremony the captain of the Drumenny team stepped up to raise the cup aloft but the crowd would have none of it. The captain was Battler Doherty and he was not the popular choice as man of the match.

"CHOOKEE BIRDEE! CHOOKEE BIRDEE!" came a mighty roar and Robin was pushed forward to receive the trophy. He and the cup were paraded round the field on the shoulders of the delirious pupils and at one point Robin thought he saw his grandfather with his arm around the shoulders of his very tearful mother but he was whizzed out the gate and up the main street so he wasn't quite sure.

Later that night there was a bit of a celebration in the Bradley house. Hugh was a very genial host and his daughter Rosaleen was piling plates with Tandoori chicken legs and cocktail sausages. Claire and Aggie Scroggy were there and Tom was listening to Lambeg as once again he relived the last ten minutes of the match over a frothing glass of black liquid.

Aileen was in Robin's room rummaging through boxes and ooing and aahing over their contents. Together they began to stick up posters and arrange trophies. They were really enjoying themselves and in a short while the room began to look cosy and lived in.

"What I can't understand," said Robin as he hammered in a nail for a framed autographed picture of the Manchester United team, "is that not once did they stand up for me in school and then they start cheering for me at a football match."

"Maybe that's it," said Aileen. "They were safe there in a big crowd and out in the open. In school, if anyone didn't do what Battler said then they would be for it later. Maybe all along they didn't like what the gang did to you and me but it was easier to say nothing or even to join in."

Robin cocked an eyebrow and looked quizzical.

"Oh, I can't explain what I'm trying to say," said Aileen, "but I remember the first time you came into the classroom. I was glad they had somebody else to tease besides me. I suppose we're all bit selfish; we all see to ourselves."

"Do you think," asked Robin, "they'll leave me in peace for a while now?"

Aileen burst out laughing. "You'll be the craze of the school. You'll have to go round all the classrooms with the cup and the *Derry Journal* will be in to take your photo."

"Three more months to go," sighed Robin, "and then we'll be free! It has been some year hasn't it?"

"It's not over yet," grinned Aileen.

Also by Poolbeg

The Pit of the Hell Hag

By

Mary Regan

When Aileen Kennedy finds a tiny two-faced figurine, the Brod of Bres, on a deserted beach near her house, she and her best friend Robin Drake are drawn into the otherworld – a world which exists alongside our own. There they meet Mathgen, the chief Druid of the Tuatha De Danaan, and the evil sorceress, the Morrigan.

As Samhain, or Hallow E'en, draws near, the Morrigan's magic is at its strongest. She wants to steal the powerful Brod because it can be used to open the Eye of Balor, the source of all evil. Aileen and Robin join the weird and wonderful beings of Mathgen's world to battle against the vile creatures of the Morrigan's underworld.

When Aileen is taken prisoner in the Pit of the Hell Hag, the Morrigan has the Brod in her grasp. Will Robin be able to stop the Morrigan and save Aileen?

Also by Poolbeg

The Red Stone of the Curses

By

Mary Regan

When Aileen Kennedy finds a riddle in an old book given to her by Robin Drake's grandfather, her blood runs cold. She realises that the riddle could be instrumental in opening the Eye of Balor, the source of all evil. Aileen knows that the Brod of Bres, the tiny two-faced figurine she found on the beach, is the key that will open the Eye. Once opened, the Morrigan, the evil Shape-shifter, and her underworld creatures will rule.

Before the children have time to warn Mathgen, the chief Druid of the Tuatha De Danaan, the sorceress steals the riddle and soon has her hands on the Brod. The race is on – whoever solves the riddle will discover the whereabouts of the Evil Eye and learn when and how the Brod can be used to open it.

In the exciting conclusion to the Brod of Bres Trilogy, the children embark on a terrifying journey in which the forces of Light and Dark gather in one final, monumental battle.

Also by Poolbeg

Shiver!

Discover the identity of the disembodied voice singing haunting tunes in the attic of a long abandoned house . . .

Read about Lady Margaret de Deauville who was murdered in 1814 and discover the curse of her magic ring . . .

Who is the ghoulish knight who clambers out of his tomb unleashing disease and darkness upon the world?

Witness a family driven quietly insane by an evil presence in their new house . . .

What became of the hideous voodoo doll which disappeared after Niamh flung it from her bedroom window?

An atmospheric and suspense-filled collection of ghostly tales by fifteen of Ireland's most popular writers: Rose Doyle, Michael Scott, Jane Mitchell, Michael Mullen, Morgan Llywelyn, Gretta Mulrooney, Michael Carroll, Carolyn Swift, Mary Regan, Gordon Snell, Mary Beckett, Eileen Dunlop, Maeve Friel, Gaby Ross and Cormac MacRaois.

Each tale draws you into a web at times menacing, at times refreshingly funny.

Also by Poolbeg

The Secret of Yellow Island

By

Mary Regan

*The Spirits of the past have risen at
last to do battle with the spirit that is
ageless – the spirit of evil.*

When Eimear Kelly arrives in Donegal to
spend the summer with her eccentric granny,
Nan Sweeney, she is not prepared for the
adventure about to unfold.

Who is the frightening giant of a man Eimear
christens 'the Black Diver' who has rented her
gran's holiday cottage? What is his dark secret
and why is he poking about the deserted
island of Inishbwee?

When Eimear meets Ban Nolan, a mysterious
old woman, and discovers the legend of the
Spanish sea captain, she is drawn into many
exciting and dangerous encounters.

The Secret of Yellow Island is a story of a
strange and unforgettable summer holiday.